Bound by the Blood Moon

A WEREWOLF SHIFTER PARANORMAL ROMANCE

THE LUNAR PROPHECY SERIES

JANAE

GOLDEN PHOENIX PUBLISHERS LLC

This book is dedicated to my best friends who spurred me on Mindy Mellott, Jan and Leigh-Ann Rodney. I'm crazy and they let me be my crazy self. You guys are my life blood whenever I feel down on my writing or myself you guys lift me up and keep me going.

A special shout out goes to my Alpha reader Keziah who always keeps me going. I cannot say enough about her keeping me focused and bouncing with me all the time. It has helped shape this book into what it has become.

To my beta readers who are the best and have helped me smooth this out to the best of their abilities: Kyla Taylor, Ariel Staniszewski, Alissa DeRouchie, and Tota Shedam. I love you all and thank you from the bottom of my heart. It has been a hard few weeks of this, but the finished product is great.

And finally, this book is dedicated to those writers out there that are afraid of publishing your first book. It is hard to know when is the right time but look deep in your soul and ask yourself if not now then why?

Coming Soon!

Visit my website to find out what is happening with my latest books, sneak peeks, and giveaways! This is a series, and the next installment will be coming out in three weeks. Stay tuned!
Sign up for my author newsletter today!
www.janaewritesbooks.com

The Blue Flame Witch Series

The Witches Prophecy: Some Legends are True

Preface

Hello Dear Reader!

Welcome to the world of Evernite! Buckle up, this is about to be a bumpy road. Before you embark on this book, I would like to let you know that this book is a part of a serial series. Don't know what that is? Don't worry, I didn't either. If you go around on the internet and question it you'll find a bunch of answers. On Wattpad or Kindle Vella you might be misled because some people say that it isn't Chapters broken up or what have you but that is what you see.

What I have done is made a bite size book that is complete but dependent on another book to make a complete story. I have heard it said that serial series is like The Last Airbender the TV series. While a novel is like a 2-3 hour movie. So I went with that. You can consume my book in a day if you want and I will be putting it out another in three more weeks. Why three weeks? I wanted to give you the best product I can give you. If you know anything about serial you know that the episodes are as larger or smaller than mine and come out frequently.

WHY AM I DOING THIS?

You'll never guess but I want to build a fan base for my

work. Well isn't that what every author wants? Not always. But I can only speak for myself. I want input. I want to hear from you. You heard me! What do you think will happen next? Did the plot twist get you? Have I pissed you off? Get on your keyboard and write to me. My email address is Janaec@janaewritesbooks.com or go to my website janaewritesbooks.com and tell me what you think. I want to hear from you.

I love to talk. And I look forward to talk to you. And sign up for my newsletter. Go on! It won't hurt. I write all the time. I have a notebook full of books I have to write. Do you want to read more? Do you have a suggestion for the next book? It might end up in there, you never know.

Anyway, I will get out of the way and let you read. I hope you enjoy this world and want to stay. Until next time, keep reading.

Janae

CHAPTER 1
The Encounter

Violet

Three days before the full moon

Run!

They say love is all butterflies and rainbows, but after the heartbreaks, ghostings, and situationships people went through, I say love can kick rocks.

Case in point--tonight.

Every girl wants to interest a prince or a king, right? Nope. I was fine just keeping to myself, caring for my pig of a father, writing in my downtime, but he just had to marry me off. And all without my input, but that was to be expected from the man.

Now here I was, running for my damn life on this chilly night in Evernite. I mean, even for this time of year, it was cold. And all I was wearing was thin, white, tight, frilly cloth held together with stitching. I was damn near bursting out of the top.

It was supposed to be a simple dinner with friends; how could that go wrong?

Dinner? What was on the menu? Me?

The demand I wear this dress should have tipped me off. I'd stupidly gone along with it, as I didn't want to be a terrible guest. It wasn't until later that I noticed all the leather. Yes. Leather. Like a damn S&M shop threw up in there. The guise of dinner was quickly squashed when someone brought out the humans, and the attending vampires began feeding from them along with me. I guess I should have been flattered the king wanted my blood. But I wasn't.

I won't put faith in a man again! And I'll never trust a damn vampire from this day on.

I glanced to the sky, Mother Moon's glow teasing me through shifting clouds.

If you get me out of this, I'll obey your will. I mean it!

Yes. I'd said that before, but... well....

I stumbled for the hundredth time, this dress a frilly silken nightmare for this escapade. Behind me, King Lysander's gothic castle loomed, and his back gardens led into the woods were rocky enough.

Oh, Goddess, I should've planned this better. But who could have predicted my moment's approach? Able to escape under the guise of having to pee. What do you do but get out by any means necessary?

I tripped again, but it wasn't a complete fall—a slip. My breath escaped in hurried puffs, and my chest heaved frantically.

I was too lost in my thoughts. And those had vanished as well. My father said I had fallen and hit my head. But there was no telling with that man. Like I remembered I'm a witch, but was my mother? Why couldn't I recall our lives together at all?

I fumbled a minute, just long enough to determine my next direction, and pushed forward. The delicate shoes, an ill-suited choice for this chase, felt like a perpetual headache on my petite feet, and my heart lurched at every stumble. I prayed these fragile heels wouldn't shatter.

Go!

My heart pounded relentlessly in my chest; it echoed in my ears. I could still hear them. Imagine them there. Was it still going on? Should I chance a glance behind me? I swear their breath was on the nape of my neck, but that was impossible.

Vampires didn't need to breathe.

Another stumble provides a chance for them to gain ground.

Fuck it!

I tossed my long, black hair out of my eyes and glanced into the darkness. The moonlight highlighted them, four foul bloodsuckers hot on my heels. They moved in a blur—nary a word between them, no sound at all except for the rustle of leaves.

My thoughts quickly shifted to my dreaded state. What would my father do now? What would Lysander do? I couldn't remember much, but the girls in my village talked uninhibited. Though the treaty of no mixing between factions was in effect, apparently, a girl could dream. And what was the dream—to be crowned a princess or queen? No sir. Not when the prince or king was a damn vampire.

Those girls giggled, sighed, and described the vampire king with a dreamy look on their faces. King Lysander had pale, life-less skin, which could be sexy. His piercing brown eyes and long, flowing blonde hair apparently made him a 'catch.' What they didn't talk of was his kinky disposition!

I stopped at the fork, unsure which direction to take.

Forward could likely be certain death--the foreboding hill loomed ahead, a dangerous cliff overlooking the churning river below.

My legs ached, my feet were pinched, and my lungs burned, urging me to keep moving. But one wrong step could end it all. The full moon peeked through billowing clouds, offering little guidance.

"Which way?" I whispered. A memory of beautiful women unlocked in my head, instructing me to wait for a sign. Were they other... witches?

So I took a hopeful minute and waited. Silence answered, and I was running out of time. With no clear path in sight, I faced an impossible choice: turn left into shadowy unknowns or right into moonlit threats?

"Get her!" a guard yelled. One lunged for me, scaring me half to death. Those jokers moved fast. I shrieked and dove away, just evading his grasp. Another sprang upon my prone position---but I was ready. Using my telekinesis, I paused him and hurled the vampire into the trees as if he were mere lint. I was always a fast learner, and moving things with my mind was easy.

But I had no time to pat myself on the back. Scrambling, I charged forward, surging ahead of the three remaining guards. I hoped the one I tossed was the commander; he was a dick, and he looked at me like I was meat the whole night.

I wanted to stop again and remove these damnable shoes, but I didn't dare. The path ahead led to only one conclusion, and I couldn't bear to dwell on it. So, I ran.

A grasp of my arm made me whirl around; my heart jumped in my chest. It was one of those bloodsuckers.

"No!" I shrieked, channeling my power to send him careening into the distance. With the threat momentarily averted, I pressed forward. Just as I sprinted away, another vampire seized my flowing sleeve, tearing the daring dress that clung to my large breasts. The rip offered some relief as my bosom found room to breathe, but this exposed even more cleavage. Gritting my teeth, I gathered my skirts and continued to climb. There was no turning back.

The cliff allowed me a break, momentarily, from fear. I was more powerful, but my limit had always been my imagination.

Lost in my thoughts again, I nearly tumbled from the abyss! A few stones from under my shoes fell hundreds of feet below. I didn't know why I stopped. I guess the reality of the situation gave me pause.

What if I hit my head, leaving me injured and vulnerable in this treacherous situation? Exposed and bleeding? I'd be an irresistible feast for the bloodthirsty vampires! No––Lysander had been quite clear. His minions were not to touch or sample me on threat of death. Vampire death was a hell of its own.

"Violet, I understand your needs perfectly," Lysander remarked at dinner, his tone unwavering. "You are a proud woman, and though your father phrased it differently, I discerned his meaning right away." He continued, "Thus forth you are to dress elegantly, obey my wishes, and cater to my desires. I trust even you can do that." A warning followed, "If not, I will exact my brand of punishment. I'm sure you'd eventually derive pleasure from it..." Right before he'd fed from me. He laughed at my disgust. All his guests had.

"Oh yes, I will have fun breaking you in, my love," — those were the final words before I escaped.

Bastards. All men are bastards out for one thing and one thing alone.

"Violet Belladonna, halt! You don't know what you are doing," one of those pricks behind me said.

I turned to him and scoffed. "I'm not a sexual toy to be passed about like I've got no soul. And I don't want to die."

"We're not dead; we're undead. You've been told this

before. Now, step away from the edge towards us," another said, beckoning to me.

I slipped off the pinching shoes, and relief washed over my whole body. I turned and faced the river.

"You insipid woman, you don't know what you're doing!" the same vampire said, looking quite comical with his made-up face. He was more feminine than I was. All those vampires were.

I tossed my hair over my nearly naked shoulder and smiled. "The name's Violet and I always know what I am doing."

I defied the 'no's' echoing behind me and plunged into the harrowing gap between the cliffs. The descent was thrilling and endless, an exhilarating free fall stretching forever. I'd done it––made it safely into the center.

However, my euphoria was short-lived. The river approached with terrifying speed, far faster than I had anticipated. Panic surged. I didn't know the water's depth! In a last-ditch effort to save myself, I tried adjusting my angle, but it was too late.

Splash! I crashed into the water at an awkward incline. The violent collision was akin to slamming one's body against an unyielding wall. The reverberation had me clenching my teeth.

Every muscle ached, and my determination to survive overpowered the searing pain. Kicking frantically, I struggled to reach the surface. My skirts tangled around my legs. Panic surged as water filled my mouth. All looked lost. Yet, just then, my head broke free to the surface. I gasped the air. It surged painfully into my lungs. I gulped. More water poured in, and my blurry vision tried to adjust.

Oh shit!

The relentless current had carried me straight into jagged rocks. I braced for the impact, but not before my head struck something unforgivingly solid. And just like that, I was knocked unconscious.

Cole

Down the river
Bloodmoon Brotherhood Camp

Why did he die so young?
The thought teased my mind without a definitive answer. My frustration could only be directed at myself that investigations weren't moving on the subject. I was so busy with my duties as the Alpha. My father's business was so complicated. When he'd met his untimely demise, the pact had given me the title, whether I earned it or not.

I hiked through the woods with practiced quiet. It was necessary to hunt the game in these woods. The thirty men with me were silent as well. I'd put off the hunt for as long as possible, and now it was do or die.

"Hey Cole! How much longer, huh? I have a nice piece waiting for me in the stead. Don't punish us because you can't get any!" Rhys called out. All the gang laughed.

I sighed, but a chuckle escaped me as well. It was his favorite thing to tease me with--the Alpha with no mate. Though I had plenty of good, lustful women who would assume the role, I waited for the perfect one.

"That's your problem, Rhys. You think too much with the head between your legs and not the one on your neck. How does your 'piece' like all your scars?" I asked.

"She thinks they're sexy. Hey, she's got friends. I'll put in a good word for you," Rhys said.

I was just about to lead them across the Moonbeam River when I got a whiff of something... different. A haunting fragrance that danced on my senses and had my head swimming in a dizzying desire. I shook it. This wasn't like me at all. Was it perfume, a flower, some unseen, unknown danger? I halted the irritable pack.

"What now, mighty leader?" Rhys grumbled from the back.

I ignored him, tuning my ears for beyond our location. My nose detected that scent again. It was alluring, and that was bad. I suspected it was a trap for someone, but who?

"Cole, are you alright?"

I turned my head and gazed at my best friend, Rafe. He'd been in the back, too. He stood tall and robust, his unruly brown hair a wild mane. It framed thoughtful brown eyes. Rafe's countenance was often serious.

Rafe, Rhys, and I had grown up together, sharing our foundational years. While Rhys had been dismissive, fueled by anger over my rapid ascent to manhood after my father's death, Rafe had congratulated me and welcomed my leadership. Even when I'd gone to him with my questions and doubts, he'd reassured me I was honest, brave, and loyal, everything needed in an Alpha. He offered guidance and support during the trying times.

"I smell something, do you?" I said.

Rafe paused, closed his eyes, and inhaled deeply. He frowned before opening his lids. "What is that?"

Alarm entered my heart. "It might be a trap. Everyone wait here."

"No, man! We should come with you...." Rhys began, his usual challenge. I hadn't noticed his presence nearer, something I usually did.

"No! That's an order."

The subordinate wolf frowned at me but held his tongue. Not dwelling on him, I hastened away. My eyes scanned the surroundings, though I didn't know what I sought. I walked on as the river diverted, leading around a treacherous bend. The closer I drew, the more potent the mysterious scent became. It was a sweet beguiling that tantalized my senses. Shivers coursed through me. I was compelled to understand this profound effect, why anticipation tingled my being. Then, I heard it.

A tiny cough.

Instinct urged me to scramble over the treacherous rocks. There, on the other side, a figure draped over the riverbank. Without hesitation, I waded through swift waters, mindful of slippery stones. Dark hair veiled the person's face--or was it a humanoid? Concerned for their breathing, I gently pushed the hair aside, revealing their face.

I discovered a young maiden. A grievous gash marred her forehead, stirring my concern. With great effort, I reached out, carefully pulling her from the precarious edge. I cradled her petite, fragile form. She was incredibly gorgeous, a vision of delicate grace, unlike any woman I'd seen.

I hastened to the river's safer side, kneeling to lay her on the ground. Placing my ear to her chest, I listened for her heartbeat's reassuring rhythm. It pulsed solid and healthy, drawing a relieved sigh from my lips. However, that enigmatic scent still enveloped her, clinging like a beguiling shroud. Her dress left little to the imagination.

This had become bigger than me, and I would need to explain it to the others. Yet, I couldn't leave her. The woods held far more terrifying dangers than werewolves on moonlit nights.

Once more, I cradled her in my arms. She coughed up water, signifying life's return. Her long lashes fluttered, and delicate lids slowly lifted. Those beguiling dark blue eyes bordering on purple stared at me momentarily. But soon, panic and fear filled her lovely gaze.

"Help me..." she whispered, grimacing as though in pain.

I gazed into those enchanting eyes and inquired, "Who are you? Where are you from?"

She began to open her mouth as if to speak. But before words emerged, she passed out once more. Another exhale. The little voice in my head warred with itself, but I wouldn't abandon her. A peculiar, captivating sensation enveloped my heart, an emotion I'd never known. Moonlight shone upon her face, making her appear hypnotically dreamlike.

"Brother, are you okay?"

I started at the sudden sound of Rafe's occurrence behind me. Turning swiftly, I noticed the group of men approaching. They had all hurried over upon catching sight of her, and an excited commotion ensued as they jostled one another for a better view of the mysterious woman in my arms.

"Back off the lot of you! Give her room to breathe," I yelled at them.

"Eh, I see what took you so long now. Did this lass fall from the sky?" Rhys asked and laughed at his joke.

"Or swam up from the sea?" Alden asked. He was younger by two years, but brave and intelligent. All the men laughed except Rafe, of course.

"Where did she come from?" he asked.

"She was lying on the other side of the river. She's hurt. I'm taking her back to the compound for care."

"Wait! She could be a human spy for the vampires! Nope, never trust a human, they say," Rhys lamented.

"So, I should just leave her to die?" I snarled, unable to stop the creeping anger that flashed in my brain.

"If that's the way Mother Moon wants it, man..."

"You bastard, you'd leave your mother to rot."

"My mother has enough sense not to fuck around in werewolf territory in a raging river in her nightgown. Back me up, Rafe," Rhys said.

Rafe looked at me, a sign he would side with me.

"Aww, you guys are making a mistake!" Rhys said, and he stomped off.

"It's your call. What do you say?" Rafe said.

"We're taking her," I said.

He nodded, and as one, everyone turned, following Rhys' lead.

I took a step, ready to assume my place among them, but an unfathomable sensation held me back. I turned and glanced over my shoulder. There, within the brush, closer than I would have preferred, a pair of ice-cold eyes burned for a fleeting moment before vanishing into the darkness.

I frowned. No other creatures were supposed to be on our lands. It was written in our treaty.

Cole!

I pivoted in the direction of the voice. Nothing.

I frowned and looked at the woman in my arms.

The moonlight grew brilliant, casting otherworldly light on her pale skin. It glowed bright. Brighter. Brightest. Darkness swept me into a vision. I stood in a strange, mystical forest. Ancient trees with shimmering silver leaves surrounded me. Wildflowers' scent filled the air, and a distant wolf howled. As I ventured deeper, a breathtaking, glowing figure appeared. Reminiscent of the woman in my arms, she extended her hand. I grabbed it.

Emotions and images rushed, flooding my mind. Her life

zipped past, too quick to grasp. One thing burned into memory——a crescent moon's smile.

I snapped back, heart pounding. This woman's arrival had brought an enigmatic twist, both a blessing and a curse. Our lives now took an unknown path. But gazing at her delicate features, it was as if she held the key to hidden worlds, a secret we were about to uncover together.

CHAPTER 2

The Mystery Unfolds

Though night was upon us, we wolves were just getting started. The village bustled with life as women, older males, and children did their respective tasks. Women gathered for gossip and to finish daily chores. Older males discussed war and tradition in loud clusters. Children snuck from their beds to play in the moonlight. Their jubilant giggles and joyous laughter punctuated the night.

The village itself exuded an aura of timelessness. Ancient trees with gnarled branches stretched over the cobblestone paths. They provided a timeline for our peaceful existence on these lands. Huts and cottages dotted the landscape, each with its own unique character. Their thatched roofs and wooden beams attested to the rich history that permeated this place. In the heart of the village, a modest square served as a gathering point. A grand, ancient oak tree stood at its center. Its branches reached skyward as though trying to touch the heavens. In the moonlight, the village took on a surreal quality. It invoked a sense of serenity and unity. This was a place where tradition and community bonds were revered.

"He's back! Cole's back!" a child yelled. Everyone cheered and headed our way.

I smiled as I observed my brethren. Their presence was a testament to the way of life in the kingdom of Evernite. Here, we were known as the Bloodmoon Brotherhood, a close-knit pack. We assembled within our villages.

Evernite was a realm that played host to an array of super-natural beings. These included witches, werewolves, fairies, and more. This mystical kingdom maintained a delicate balance of harmony. Each faction resided in relative isolation from the others. This measure aimed at preserving the peace. Despite our differences, we recognized the importance of coex-istence and cooperation. Evernite was a place where diversity thrived. We all respected the boundaries that allowed us to live side by side. This fostered an enduring sense of unity within our respective communities.

"Where is he? Where is Cole?" an elder yelled, milky eyes searching our group.

I was aware my pack would have questions. Their leader's actions tonight would raise concerns. We never took in strangers, especially so close to the full moon.

I stepped through the crowd. The men parted for me as I approached our eldest, Magnus. He stood with the other elders. They looked on with frowning faces. That didn't worry me––they always sported downturned expressions.

"Who is she? Human?" Magnus asked. He was shorter than me. His dome was bare, but he boasted hair everywhere else––white hair.

"I do not know, Magnus, but she is hurt. I could not leave her," I said.

Magnus nodded and beckoned me to follow.

"Let us hope your big heart will not lead us astray, pack leader," Agnus, another elder, said. He was taller, with grey hair and barely any teeth. He scowled, but he meant it.

Magnus guided us to my hut. It became mine after my father passed away three months ago. My mother ushered me inside.

Belinda Wilderwolf retained her timeless beauty, her tall figure resembling a graceful Willow tree. A long braid of brown hair hung to waist level, a subtle hint of gray near her temple. Her attire comprised a traditional dress fashioned from Hallobear skin. Her tawny-colored cloth shoes reached midway on her calves.

I gently laid her on my bed, noticing her worrying pallor.

"Where is Camille?" my mother said.

"I am here, Mother Belinda." A small, dark-haired girl, her locks as black as the night and eyes of deep brown, almost matching in shade, squeaked with a bubbly smirk on her lips. She entered the room with a bowl filled with a solution and several cloths in her arms.

Following her, Ellis, the healer, shuffled in. He had a decade's seniority over my twenty-three years. His eyes lingered on the beauty resting on my bed.

He raised an inquisitive brow. "Human?"

"I do not know," I answered, but there was bite to my tone.

After Ellis had ogled her for an indecent amount of time, he glanced at my frowning face and cleared his throat.

Ellis and I turned away out of respect until my mother informed us the girl was ready for examination. Ellis diligently went about his duties, tending to the visible wounds. Her side bore severe bruising, displaying a horrible purplish hue against her pale skin.

"Hey Cole, you see this?" Ellis said.

I furrowed my brow and took a step closer. She lay on her back, her breasts covered by bandage cloth. Ellis delicately rolled her over to expose her lower half. She wore silken white panties, but that wasn't what immediately caught my attention. It was the medium-sized, sideways crescent moon birthmark on her lower back. The mark curved inward, resembling a gentle smile. My face remained firm, but it was the same etching in her skin I'd seen in my vision.

"What does it signify?" I asked.

"Hmm," Ellis said and ran his fingertips over the mark.

My muscles tensed, though I couldn't explain why. My mother seized my arm, guiding me from the hut to the adjacent one. She compelled me to sit on her bed and turned to leave. Before she closed the door behind her, she raised a warning finger, her unspoken message clear.

I longed to pace. What did it all mean? Of course, I didn't. The prospect of an impending earful from my mother prevented me from disobeying. So, I sat there with my arms crossed.

I couldn't help but think about the girl and whether Ellis was becoming interested in her. The thought furrowed my brows. But I chided my imagination for running wild. He wouldn't. Would he? Still, a nagging doubt lingered.

Ellis had lost his Elena during childbirth just last spring. He had remained a composed and wise choice in our village. I felt a prickling of jealousy.

Two minutes later, my mother entered with a bowl of Hallobear beef stew––a hearty meal. The Hallobear were formidable foes; their meat was a unique treat. She handed it to me, and though I almost refused, she raised a questioning brow that made it clear I should comply. I consumed the delicious meal in just a few bites. I licked the remnants from my lips.

"So, you're enamored. But what do you know of her?" she said.

"How?" I raised my brows.

"A mother knows. Don't worry; no one would suspect. I know my baby."

I chuckled. "She was washed up on the side of the river. Do you think she will survive?"

My mother smiled, and her entire face brightened. "Yes, baby. Ellis is good. She may look worse than she is."

Relief washed over my whole body.

"You should be prepared to address the concerns of the people. They'll want to know what is going on."

I nodded. There was a knock on the door.

"Come in!" my mother said.

Ellis shuffled in, looking older than he was. "I've healed her as much as I can. There was a gash to her head, and her stomach was bruised, but other than that, she seemed okay. She needs rest."

"Then rest she shall get." I stood and stretched.

"But..." he said.

"But what?" I asked.

"She's been fed from. Vampire bite."

I looked at my mother, who'd brought her hand to her mouth.

"Um... the people are asking questions. I think you should come out and talk to them."

"We will be out shortly, Ellis," my mother said with another breathtaking smile.

He nodded and left.

She turned to me. "Do you know what you're going to say?"

"Yes. The truth," I said.

"Good. Your father would be so proud, baby. I know I am."

I walked over to her and wrapped my arms around her warmly. Afterward, we set off for the center of the camp—a brisk walk through the endless rows of homes, then onto the town's square. There was more land than we knew what to do with. The wild game ran untamed on our lands. Bushes and trees provided plenty of vegetables and fruit a plenty.

My thoughts wandered to the Vampire King and his faction during the journey. It had been a long while since we'd heard a peep from them. Not since my father had initiated a peace treaty with them many moons ago.

As we exited into the meeting area, about a hundred wolves had gathered, engaged in collective conversation. I leaped up onto the makeshift stage, constructed from wood, and raised me about a foot off the ground. The crowd slowly hushed, and their eager gazes fixated on me, awaiting what I had to say.

"Hail Bloodmoon Brotherhood and hail Mother Moon!" I said first.

"Hail, brother! Hail Mother Moon," everyone said.

"Hail! Hail!" the children squeaked, and they giggled. The older wolves laughed at them.

"I know you all have questions. I will answer as many as possible," I said.

A young woman named Otta raised her hand.

I nodded to her.

"Who is she? Like a princess?"

"I know little about her. I found her along the river bank. She was alone."

Another man raised his hand; he was one of the elders. "Are we safe? Could she be a spy? Like from the vampires?"

I frowned. "Where did you hear that?"

The man's expression initially held fear, and he glanced at Rhys, who sat with a beautiful, curvy girl on his lap. Another young girl sat at his side. They were engaged in whispered conversations and giggles. They existed in their bubble. I audibly cleared my throat, capturing the trio's attention. They snapped to, their expressions shifting from guilt to surprise.

"As far as I know, she has not proven to be a spy. But if she is found to be, she will be dealt with accordingly."

"Where will she stay?" This came from Camille. She smiled and giggled. The little minx knew the answer; she wanted me to tell the clan.

"Right now, she is in my hut, where she will remain until we find her shelter."

"Will she stay here, or are we sending her home?" Rhys asked.

"That will depend on her. Look, guys, right now, she's dead to the world and all alone. Imagine your mothers, sisters, or daughters out there in her state. What would you do? Would you throw her out alone or care for her?" I asked, trying to appease them. The concerned look on their faces reassured me.

"She'll bring doom to us. This goes against tradition––no strangers. Leave her to her own devices. She's not our problem. We need food, not another mouth to feed!" Agnus groused.

"You eat enough for two. It's no wonder you're complaining of food," my mother said.

"She's bringing death with her. That girl's trouble, she's been fed on! The vampires are going to bring in death and seal all our fates!" Agnus warned.

Dammit!

Everyone shouted at once. The children began crying and screaming for their mothers.

"Everyone, calm!" I rumbled over the din.

Everyone looked at me.

I sighed. "Yes. She's been bitten, but she's not yet turned."

"But she is beautiful. They will come for us! Be warned, *mighty leader*!" Agnus said in a condescending tone.

"That's enough! Everyone, go back to what you were doing. I'll handle the girl," I declared, my voice firm and commanding.

I left the group and headed to my hut with a determined stride. Agnus had been an insufferable provocateur, always opposing my family's leadership within the clan. He had deemed me too weak to rule even as a baby, as though you could tell at that age. My father told me. All my life, I exceeded expectations to prove that bastard wrong.

I jerked open the door of my hut and entered swiftly. I hovered over the young girl, who appeared frail and innocent. It was perplexing how so much trouble could stem from her.

Suddenly, she frowned and shook her head. The apparent turmoil in her dreams caused her current distress. She moaned and began fighting against an unseen adversary, her movements growing increasingly agitated. Alarmed, I rushed to her side. As though attending to a pup, I gently touched her arms. However, when I felt her cool skin, a strange energy coursed through my hands. In an instant, I snatched my hands away. Still, she continued to struggle, begging someone in her dreams.

I tried again, leaning in and murmuring soothing words, "Shh! Shh! It's okay, love. Calm down; you are safe."

Within seconds, she calmed, her furrowed brows smoothing out as her agitation subsided. She grew still once more. Her restful state elicited a sigh of relief from me.

I fetched a dark brown fur blanket from the foot of the bed and settled into a comfortable chair in the corner of my hut, pulling the blanket around myself as I tried to rest. Somehow, the whole exertion had left me exhausted. I resolved one fact: this girl was special. Special indeed.

Hours later....

*I*t was a dream because my father stood before me. In fact, all my forefathers were there, gazing upon me with solemn eyes and gentle smiles. As I walked past them, they nodded in approval. I continued to march towards the radiant golden altar, which stood bare, save for the unearthly gleam of light that emanated from it.*

"Cole Wilderwolf, do you know why you are here?" a lilting voice asked.

"No."

"Do you know who I am?" the voice asked.

"Yes, you are Mother Moon."

"Good. The girl needs your protection now. Your fates are entwined."

"Who is she?"

"She is the bringer of peace for your people."

"What is her name?"

"That is not important. For now, know that I have spoken. Heed my words, for they will keep your people safe. I must go now. Remember."

"Mother. Mother wait! Mother Moon!"

The landscape began merging with itself like an ice cream melting and mixing into brown sludge. It was maddening until everything faded into white....

A loud gasp woke me. I looked around in the dark. The weak morning light rays cast on the girl as she sat up, looking around. I hurried over to her. My head swam in liquid bliss when I got within inches of her. I shook it.

She eyed me with extensive, frightened eyes. I relaxed my face and tried to calm my thumping heart. We stared at each other for a moment. She still wore the bandages over her bosom, and it heaved as she panted.

"Who are you?" she asked.

"My name is Cole. I am the pack leader here. What is your name?" I whispered.

"My name?" She frowned, and a dip appeared in her sooty brows. "My name? I-I-I don't know. Where am I?"

"You're in my hut. You are safe. Do you not know who you are?"

"Your hut? Am I your wife?"

"No, love. I found you by the river. You were hurt."

"River? Hurt?" she repeated. Her hand raised to her head, where a bandage covered her wounded forehead. She slowly pulled her hand away and stared at it.

I frowned. "Are you in pain? Would you like for me to get someone..." I began to rise, but she suddenly reached out and grabbed my arm in a firm grip. Again, a spark crackled between us. Panic darkened her beautifully blue eyes to a deeper violet.

"Please don't go. I-I-I am scared."

I nodded. "Okay. I will stay. You don't have to worry. No one will harm you here."

She nodded, watching me with those luminous purple eyes. I waited for her to lie back, but she remained sitting up.

"Would you like to get up? Maybe have some food?" I asked.

She shook her head, frowning.

"Would you like more sleep?"

She nodded. Again, I waited for her to lay back. She did move but pushed over as if making a space for me. She waited. I climbed into the enormous bed with her and laid on my back. She lay down again, putting her head on my chest instead of the pillow.

"Thank you. I dreamed of you..." she whispered and sighed. I wrapped my arms around her, and a burgeoning emotion ensnared my heart when I did. Powerful emotions surged through my body, not limited to physical.

Protect her, a voice whispered in my head.

She snuggled into my arms, slamming me back into reality. While she slid her hand across my bare chest, electricity crackled and sparked so loudly and vividly that I swore I could see it. I frowned. My mind was playing tricks on me. Wasn't it?

Her scent ensnared me again. This time, physically, I began to harden. I cleared my throat. I didn't want to admit it, but an undeniable force drew me to her. It was more authentic than if someone had declared it. Somehow, deep within me, My mind and soul confirmed it. This girl was my fated mate.

CHAPTER 3
Complications

<u>Violet</u>

The sensation was utterly indescribable—a swirling mixture of pain and exquisite pleasure. I struggled to comprehend the immediacy of it all. The man... The man with long, flowing black hair and eyes as deep and mesmerizing as the sea. He stood as the largest man I had ever laid eyes on.

Although, an aura of serenity surrounded him. I found myself wondering how his face would light up with a smile. Although it already held a captivating handsomeness.

My body, an enigmatic passenger, both part of me and separate, reacted to him immediately. I couldn't recall education of its workings, but now it was alien. Maybe my mother taught me. My mother? A hazy image of a woman flashed before my mind's eye—her long, wavy black hair, warm and friendly brown eyes, and infectious smile.

A sigh escaped me but emerged as a soft moan. I lay upon something warm and covered in hair, perhaps a rug?

My eyelids fluttered, their weight making it a struggle to regain consciousness. I shifted in my toasty cocoon and tried to lift my head. It had been so long since I'd experienced this measure of coziness and safety. But how long had I been like this? My gaze dropped, and my mouth fell open. I wasn't resting on a rug; it was skin. I lay on someone––a man's chest.

With some trepidation, I raised my head and looked at him. There he was, the man from my dreams, asleep before me, vulnerable and at peace. He was a stunning figure, not much older than me. Could this man be my husband?

I attempted to recollect the events that led me here and, even more puzzling, who I was. However, my efforts were futile. I couldn't even summon my name. Frustration welled inside me. I lifted myself from his robust form with a slow, hesitant movement. His chest was broad, covered only by a simple brown vest. His darker brown pants clung to his muscular legs. I couldn't help but notice those powerful arms had been cradling me.

Something quickened in my body. A flicker... at first. A trick of light? No, I glanced at the window, where intense sunlight streamed in, casting a hazy orange glow. I looked back at the man. What was his name again? Cody? Cameron?

Absentmindedly, I drummed my fingertips. A spark ignited when I touched him. My eyes widened. My trembling fingers rested on the man's chest. I eyed him, still sleeping. I tapped his chest again. Another spark!

What the hell is going on?

Something very wrong was happening to me. Something that made me wonder about my identity even further: I didn't want to harm the man. He'd been so lovely, and he was so handsome. I gasped.

Why am I thinking about his handsomeness? I should think of a way to repay him. Well, there was one way...

"Good morning. How are you feeling?" a gentle voice said.

I still started with a tiny gasp. My cheeks warmed. I frowned because the man hadn't opened his eyes, but he sensed me. I eyed his thick lips, never remembering men with lips such as he possessed. As I gazed at him, he slowly lifted his lids, and I was captivated by the stormy depths of his blue eyes.

"I still ache, but I am better," I said. "Where am I?"

"Do you not remember our conversation?"

I frowned and tried to remember an earlier dialogue. It filtered through my mind slowly. "A little. Are you sure I am not your wife?"

A hint of a smile slightly curved his beautiful lips. "I think I would remember. Would you like a meal?"

I nodded. Unfortunately, he drew himself to a seated posture but stretched with closed eyes. My brows rose, eyeing his expanding chest. I dashed my eyes away before he finished.

He rose and turned to me. "I will return unless you want to come with me."

I pulled the blanket to cover my chest, which was almost revealed. "I'd like to stay here. I need something to wear."

He nodded and turned away. Once he left, I leaned to the bed where he'd lain and sniffed it. His scent was very male, strong, and wonderful. I rose and giggled at my stupidity. Here I was lost, alone with no memory of anything, including my name, and I was fawning over my rescuer.

But a good-looking man was a good-looking man. I giggled.

I got to my feet a bit wobbly. A frilly dress lay there, so I slid it on and stretched. It wasn't my style, but it would do for now.

I set to righting the bed. I began singing a tune that popped into my head. A haunting song about love lost and regret. As I was positioning the pillow, I heard a giggle that didn't come from me. Three pairs of eyes peered at me from a window. It was small children, so I wasn't afraid.

I feigned ignorance and continued to sing, dancing around the little hut like I was dancing with the man. I kept my voice low and spoke nonsensical to make the children laugh. I was rewarded with theirs. I finished my song and suddenly turned to them.

"Boo! I see you!" I exclaimed.

They screamed and ran away—three girls with long braids. I smiled.

"Making friends?" someone said behind me.

I gasped and turned to find the man standing there with two bowls of steaming food. A sly smirk played on his lips as he set the bowls on the table. He pulled out a chair for me. I hurried to take a seat. He pushed me in and settled beside me.

The meal looked delicious, and the scent was even more appealing. He handed me a spoon. I dug into the food that tasted of sweetened barley. I was done quicker than I anticipated.

"You have a good appetite."

I gazed into those eyes, resembling a chilly morning sky, and couldn't help but smile. He frowned. Before I could inquire why, a knock echoed at the door.

"Come in!" the man bellowed.

A petite woman with a long brown braid, sharing the same face as the man, entered the room. Her braid held strands of gray hair, unmistakably his mother. My cheeks burned as I recalled our night together. I averted my gaze from the smiling woman.

"Hello dear, my name is Belinda. I am Cole's mother. What is your name?"

My eyes remained on my lap. "I do not know, ma'am."

"Call me Lindy, and that is okay. I understand you need

some clothes. Yes, this dress will not do. Would you like to bathe, too?" Cole's mother asked.

I regarded her and nodded.

"I can show you where the riverbank is or..." She stopped and tapped her finger to her cheek. "Cole can show you."

"What?" Cole said like he hadn't been listening. He frowned at his mother.

"Oh my," I said.

"Mother, I am sure she'd like a female to show her the way--" he began.

"Nonsense. I am not suggesting you watch her. Just show her where it is."

He opened his mouth, but his mother raised her brow. They both looked at me.

My cheeks warmed considerably, but I answered and firmed my voice. "T-t-that's fine."

Lindy nodded. "Good, here is a Lyraclawn of my own. You look about my size."

She lifted a dress of sandy brown fur like the one she wore, except hers was darker brown. I accepted the beautiful clothing. She also gave me some tall shoes that were tawny brown too. They looked like they'd near my calves.

"The dress is from a young Lyraclawn. I'd hoped I'd pass it to my daughter-in-law." She sighed.

My eyes widened just as Cole said. "Mom!" sharply.

Cole's mother chuckled, and he shooed her out the door. He turned to me and rubbed the back of his neck.

"We should go," he said. I nodded, and he held the door open.

Cole

As we walked through the compound, we were quiet. The girl looked even more alluring with her eyes open, and I fought hard to keep mine from wandering.

My mother knew, but I hadn't thought she'd embarrass me like that. She was too eager to push us together, but it wasn't that simple. I still had mixed feelings about my attraction to the girl. And I was concerned about a vampire feeding on her. One bite wouldn't change her, they say. But if she received vampiric blood in return, the entire clan could be in danger.

I cleared my throat. "It's a shame you do not know your name."

"Yes, quite," she replied with an embarrassed smile.

"My mother didn't mean anything. I hope you are not embarrassed.".

She looked at me, her eyes filled with shyness and amusement. "Your mother appears quite... happy to help."

I nodded. "She can be overzealous when it comes to me," I admitted. "She means well; she just wants me to be married off."

Her gaze locked with mine, and there was uncertainty in her eyes. "I don't mind, really. I have no memory of other mothers other than my own."

I stopped walking. "You remember your mother?"

She nodded. "She died when I was younger."

"Still can't remember your name?"

She shook her head, her gaze drifting elsewhere. Biting her bottom lip, she evoked a breathless anticipation. Blinking rapidly, I seized her cool, slender hand and guided her forward.

Her smaller hand was engulfed within mine, and she responded with a reassuring squeeze.

"There's something else bothering you," she stated after we'd walked some way.

"I have to host another hunting party as the moon festival is about to happen."

"Moon festival?"

"Yes. I... we all are... um... werewolves, and the festival is part of our traditions. This time, it's during the Blood Moon, a celestial event that enhances our abilities and strengthens our connections. During the Blood Moon, werewolves undergo a profound shift, becoming more powerful and closer to our true nature. It's a time when some find their mates," I explained, my voice filled with reverence for the occasion.

"Do you have a mate?"

"I do not."

She frowned. "I thought you said you were the leader. Why does the leader not have a wife."

"I... am waiting for the right girl."

"Must she be a w-w-werewolf too?"

"It is the way."

"Oh."

She turned away and focused her gaze, and I followed her stare. We had reached the calmer side of the river, where a cluster of trees and rocks lined the edge. The trees formed a substantial thicket, offering privacy and a place to hang our clothes to keep them dry.

"This is where the women bathe. You can disrobe behind the tree and hang your clothes on the branches. I will be at the other oak; take your time."

Her gaze locked with mine. Time stood still. As the wind picked up, it carried her delicate, alluring scent toward me. I stood, captivated. With a subtle tilt of her head, her pupils dilated, revealing untold depths that threatened to harden my whole damn body. I couldn't look away. I opened my mouth but had no words. They didn't matter. I wanted this moment to last forever. But she smiled, turned, and disappeared behind the ancient tree, leaving me cold and yearning for her return.

I swallowed, attempting to divert my thoughts. I needed to focus on anything but her tempting body. My mind darted frantically from her haunting eyes to her ethereal singing, that mesmerizing melody from earlier, to the fact that she was naked.

"Ahh!"

I spun around, heart racing, and rushed toward the tree. I couldn't tell if she had sustained more injuries. My worry for her well-being consumed my thoughts.

"Are you okay?" I asked.

"Yes, it's just the water is cold. Is this soap?" she asked, her voice sounding muffled.

"Yes, near the edge. You sure you're okay?"

"Yes. I may have forgotten my name, but I remember how to bathe. I will be done soon," she promised with a laugh.

I hurried to the other large oak tree and cluster of bushes. As I disrobed, I thought about the girl, which was a mistake for obvious reasons. I grabbed the woodsy-smelling soap for us werewolf males and suds my body quickly. She was correct; the river was icy, and it did wonders for my hard-on. I didn't want the woman to think I was a fiend. But I couldn't stop wondering if her body was as silky as I imagined. Was she a screamer? Or was she a virgin?

"Cole?" came the girl's voice.

My eyes widened as I had inadvertently been stroking myself, and she sounded close.

"I-I-I'll be done soon!" I said, hoping to halt her from discovering me.

"Okay."

I quickly rinsed off and climbed out of the water. As I

dried myself, I thought of my father and the hunt. I thought of any and everything to soften my dick. I dressed quickly, not wanting to keep her waiting. If only I were Rhys and not me.

I pondered--what would my father have done? How had he won my mother? Had it been at a Moon festival like the one approaching? I smiled, picturing my parents together. A pity they'd only birthed me, leaving me siblingless.

"There you are!" the girl said with a breathtaking smile. Her eyes were clear, dark blue. She stood, dusting herself off. If she was beautiful before, now she was downright stunning. Clad in the dress, she resembled a she-wolf, exuding enchantment. Camille would be green with envy.

I approached, and her natural scent mingled with our handmade soap, titillating my senses. Wet dark hair framed her face, purple eyes gazing at me curiously, captivated by their beauty. I couldn't resist caressing her soft cheek, her eyes closing in response.

"Are you a witch?" I whispered, my words escaping before I could halt them.

Her eyelids flew open, and she frowned. "Why would you ask me that?"

"You are beguiling, but please, tell me your name."

"Call me whatever you like," she replied.

I sighed. "Come, they will expect us back soon."

I turned away, but she seized my arm. In an innocent moment, she stood on tiptoes, pecking my cheek. Something stirred deep inside. I couldn't resist taking her hand as we continued. We walked together, fingers swinging in unison.

Soon, I detected a scent - raw, unmistakable. My heartbeat quickened, and I stopped walking.

"What is it, Cole?"

"I smell..." I turned my head just as three stepped from their hiding spots. "... vampires."

All of them were garbed in a uniform of grey slacks, vests,

and frilly shirts. Their androgyny was evident with their elongated eyes, carefully painted faces, and flowing long hair.

"Boy, hand us the girl and no one gets hurt," the leader of the Vampire King's scouts said.

Cracking my neck, I pushed the girl behind me. I clenched my fists, squared my shoulders, and with a set jaw, I declared in a deep, loud voice, "She's not going anywhere. She's with me."

"You cannot claim what is not yours, boy!" the vampire said with disgust on his face.

"You do not claim a woman, you ass. You also don't come to my lands and tell me what is or is not," I said, my tone steady.

The vampire raised a perfectly made-up eyebrow. I raised mine as well. The girl clutched my vest behind me.

This was madness; I was not with this woman, but I'd be damned if I'd surrender her to these undead fiends. Somehow, she had etched her presence onto my very soul.

Stand down, Cole! Think of the loyalty to your clan! It comes before this woman.

"You dare challenge the Vampire King, boy? And what of the treaty?" he inquired, a snide smirk playing on his thin, pale lips.

"The treaty doesn't include kidnapping," I snarled.

"You dare mettle, you stinking mutt. I should cut your head off for your insolence!" he declared, drawing his long sword.

I scoffed. "Before you could even get close to one of us, you'd be dead, freak. I'm no child, and this is no game," I said, extending my hand that had partially morphed its claws.

The vampire glared, looked around me, and said, "Violet, The Vampire King has been looking for you everywhere. Come with us now!"

The girl gripped my vest and gasped.

Violet? Named after those eyes, huh?

"Are you ugly and deaf? I said she's not going anywhere. Leave now or stay and be ripped to shreds. I'm an Alpha. I do not need the moon."

"I've wasted far too much time. Hand me the girl and turn away," the vampire demanded, with a sinister edge to his voice.

"What does he want with her?" I asked.

"Learn your place! That is none of your business," the vampire spat, his tone dripping with condescension.

"I am making it my business. You are on my lands, far from home. Remember *your* place, freak!"

The one who had been speaking appeared to be giving it some thought. His gaze shifted between his men and me, a scowl deepening. "This isn't over," he grumbled. They backed away, and I kept my eyes fixed on them as they dissolved into the shadows.

I exhaled.

I pivoted toward the girl. Tears streamed down her cheeks, and her large, doe-like eyes glistened with moisture that clung to her long, dark lashes.

"Your name is Violet. Fitting," I whispered and caressed her cheek.

"I remember. I remember. Violet Belladonna, I am not from here. I am from the human village of Moorwood. I do not wish harm to come to your camp. Will you turn me away now?"

Her heartfelt cries were not ignored. My heart broke at her sorrow. I never wanted her to experience the agony she was going through ever again. I wiped the crocodile tears from her cheeks. "You do not have to leave if you don't want to. Shh! No more crying. I will protect you."

"I want to stay," she said, rushing into my arms and burying her face in my neck. "I want to stay with you."

I cradled her, providing comfort. However, a sudden twig snap broke the moment. Alden stood there. His expression clarified that he had witnessed everything. I frowned. He turned and ran away.

"Oh no! What will happen now?" she questioned.

"Shh! We will figure out a solution, love. But we've got bigger problems," I whispered.

"What?' She eyed me, her eyes filled with curiosity and concern.

"I don't think you are simply a meal. Something tells me you were promised... to the Vampire King," I confessed with dread.

CHAPTER 4

So much for true love

King Lysander

My study was quiet except for the crackling fire. Shadows danced on the stone walls, cast by the flames in the ornate marble fireplace. This cavernous room where I researched ancient texts and practiced dark rituals was in the castle's west wing, far from the chatter and frivolity that consumed the rest. Tomes stacked on mahogany shelves lined the space, containing centuries of accumulated magical knowledge. Priceless relics and artifacts decorated the study, collected over my many years. At the center sat an imposing claw-footed desk carved from ancient oak, strewn with scrolls and magical implements. My power and influence spread like tendrils from this room, controlling my vampire kingdom and beyond. Yet today, a disquieting energy pulsed through the space.

I must act swiftly to regain control before the prophecies

come to fruition. The time was near--Violet's fate and mine would soon intertwine.

"Sir?"

I lifted my gaze from my desk to my first in command--Lennox. He was capable as they came, but lately, he'd been disappointing me. Deeply disappointing me.

"Yes."

"The seer is here, sir. Forgive me, sir, but what is so special about this one."

"Violet Belladonna is powerful--and I shall control that power! That bitch doesn't know what to do with it, but I do! A war is coming, one that is for the good of our people. See that you do not disappoint me again."

"Yes, sir."

I stood, fixed my robes, and strode onward through the hall to the throne room. My attendant Seraphina hurried to my side. She was a tempting beauty--long, luscious red hair, brilliant green eyes, thick, pouty lips, and large, firm breasts. I know. It was her place to keep me satisfied until Violet returned. We'd had a grand session just last night; she enjoyed every position I'd put her into.

"Morning, Your Majesty. How are you feeling?" she cooed. Today, she wore a tight green dress that reached her ankles and green 6-inch heels.

I eyed her cleavage as it bounced joyously. "Tired. There's been no word of Violet, and if one of those mangy mutts bonds with her, it's all over."

"Don't worry, Your Highness. You will find her before then."

I stopped walking when we entered my lavish throne room. Turning to Seraphina, I seized the back of her head and kissed her plump lips. My tongue darted into her mouth, and I delighted in savoring the metallic taste of sweet blood on her tongue. One hand grabbed a handful of her bosom, and the other wrapped around her voluptuous body. She moaned, and her hand reached inside my robes to find my semi-hardened cock. She enclosed her soft hand around it and jacked me. I wanted her––against the wall. She had her other hand in my hair, and I was being driven crazy with lust. It danced in my veins; the sensation welled in my balls.

"Still lustful as ever, eh?" someone female said, and then came a smack to my ass.

I pulled away from Seraphina to gaze at Isabella, my seer. She smirked and winked. Isabella was older; how much I would never know. How old could a vampire be and still look to be in their twenties?

Isabella had dark, curly hair and brown eyes. Today, she wore a medieval-style long navy-blue dress with bell sleeves and a long black cloak. She was very frisky, as were all the women that worked for me. Oh yes! I had women on the employ, too. Their place was in the bedroom, but a casual fuck in the throne room was also delightful here and there.

I cleared my throat, righted my clothes, and strode to my chair. I sat in the lush, cushioned seat and faced the woman.

"Your Highness, I bring good news and not-so-good news."

"What is the good news?" I asked Isabella.

"You will get the upper hand. She is who you think she is. A rarity in this land."

I smiled. "Good. Now...."

"Don't you want the bad news?"

I sighed and smoothed my hair. "What is it?"

"An Alpha has claimed her."

"I know that you, insipid woman! How do I get her away from him before they mate?"

"You cannot."

"That fucker better not stick his dick in anything other

than another mutt!" I slammed my fist, creating a loud thumping echo in the room.

"I only give you the news, sire. You can call her, but she is stuck on him. I think it is true love," Isabella said.

"Love? Fuck love! They've only just met."

"Yes. Tis true, but true love transcends time."

I frowned. A tick in my eyebrow made it jump. "What does that mean?"

Isabella leaned in and raised her brows. "They've done this before."

Violet

As we returned from the river, a strange mix of emotions churned within me. The encounter with the Vampire King's men had left me unsettled and vulnerable. I did remember my escape from them the other night, the dinner and everything. I felt so bad. Here I was, making things hard for Cole, but hearing his declaration gave me goosebumps!

My newfound feelings for Cole had caught me off guard. The protectiveness he exhibited, and his unwavering determination to keep me safe all resonated deep within me. He was sincere, and that recognition frightened me almost as much as the vampires themselves. I'd sworn off men, but this was no mere man. This was an Alpha. I bit my lip. If those stupid girls could see me now.

Cole talked about the upcoming Moon Festival, explaining

the rituals and transformations that occurred under the mystical blood moon. But I found it hard to concentrate, distracted by a subtle tingling energy awakening inside me. Even just waving my hands, the air responded. It was exhilarating but terrifying.

"The blood moon heightens our abilities," Cole was saying. "We draw power from its glow. But we must also be wary of letting our wolf natures get carried away."

I nodded, only half-listening. My mind was consumed by the growing electrical hum under my skin. Could it have something to do with why the Vampire King wanted me? I delved deep into the recesses of my mind, exploring the furtive depths to string things together and make sense of it all.

I had magic within me! Cole had been correct. That thrilled me as much as it did when my father told me he knew. I'd played with it, of course, in secret. And that was what I wanted to do now. It was calling to me, telling me to come home. But would Cole turn me away if he were to know?

Cole eyed me with concern. "Are you alright? I know the vampire encounter was a shock."

"I'm fine," I assured him, smiling to hide my racing thoughts. I couldn't let anyone know about this budding sorcery, not yet.

We arrived at the compound gates where a crowd had gathered, their eyes filled with apprehension and suspicion. Protectively, Cole stepped forward to address them, deflecting their misgivings about my presence. But their doubts barely registered as I snuck away, excited to test my powers in private finally. The blood moon was awakening more than just the wolves...

As I slipped away into the woods seeking solitude, a gentle voice suddenly called out – "My dear, wait!"

I turned to Cole's mother, Belinda, hastening toward me, her brow furrowed with concern. "It's not safe to wander alone with night approaching. Please, walk with me."

Nodding, I fell into step beside her along a winding forest path. I didn't know what to do.

What should I tell her?

A comfortable silence descended, the sounds of the woodlands surrounding us.

After some time, Lindy spoke, her voice kind. "You needn't hide your talents from me, my child. I know you are special."

I froze, staring at her with wide eyes. How could she know?

Sensing my shock, she smiled. "A mother's intuition. But your secret is safe with me. When I was a young pup, they called me "Morveth" or 'big eyes' because I noticed most things others did not." My shoulders relaxed as she continued. "Our pack would not understand such gifts yet. But in time, with nurturing, your powers may save us all. For now, allow an old wolf to teach you our ways."

I found myself nodding quite at ease. "It is not only that which bothers me. When Cole and I were returning, three vampires came from the woods. They demanded Cole hand me over. Cole refused."

Lindy bobbed her head. "My son, whether he knows or does not know, has claimed you in his heart."

"Will the pack throw him out?"

"It is not our way. Leaders are chosen by birth. Only a defeat from an official duel or a declaration from Mother Moon will change tradition. A Wilderwolf has been a pack leader of the Bloodmoon Brotherhood since time began. The elders are suspicious of strangers because Evernite's peace is very fragile."

"What creatures are in Evernite?"

"Oh, all kinds, love. Fairies, witches, vampires, ghouls, werewolves, just to name a few."

"Oh my. I only found out I am a witch. How powerful could I be?"

Lindy leaned in with a sly smile. "Let's find out, shall we?"

My thoughts returned to the Vampire King, a figure of dread and mystery.

Despite these thoughts, I couldn't ignore the peculiar sensations building within me. The dormant powers that had long remained hidden were stirring back to life, which both intrigued and alarmed me. I needed to understand and control these abilities, not just for my sake, but for the sake of the man who had vowed to protect me at all costs.

"For our sake and the sake of Mother Moon's Forest, we should start small. Stand and open your hand, palms up. Feel the power within you build. Slowly draw it to you."

I stood, held out my hand, and tried to "feel" for the magic. I did it for a tense few moments, but nothing happened. Just as I was about to try a different tactic, I sighed and relaxed; only then did a crazy pull happen. It started in my navel, an irritating buzzing that grew into an itch. It traveled from my navel throughout my stomach into my chest, then my arm and hand.

"Child, open your eyes!" came Lindy's excited exclamation.

I opened my eyes to investigate my palm. A wisp of yellowish light glowed, burning as brightly as the sun, but it was not consuming my skin. A fleeting thought filtered through of turning the energy a different color, and shockingly, it changed from yellow to fuchsia to blue and back to yellow. I transferred it from one palm to the other.

"Very good, dear," Lindy said with her gorgeous smile. She stood and stretched. "Come with me."

I hurried to her side, curious. "Where are we going?"

"Now that we found out how powerful you could be, we should find out how your fate is mingled with my son's, shall we?"

A numbness mingled in my belly, and I thought I'd heave butterflies, but I followed the determined Lindy. I'd follow her anywhere.

We veered off the path through the woods. The golden leaves shimmered on the forest floor, their crunch delighting my ears. I tingled as I walked. I enjoyed the power coursing through me. It was like the good when Cole was near me. The good when I kissed him, and though I wanted more I refrained.

Lindy grabbed my hand as we got closer to a little hut sitting in between two grand trees, from the chimney plumed purple smoke. Lindy marched to the home and knocked.

The door slowly creaked open, and a considerably older woman stared at us.

"Lindy, why are you bothering me?"

"Please, Angel, we will only be but a minute."

The older woman grunted. But she shuffled away and left the door open. Cole's mother prepared to follow, but I halted her.

"Lindy, who is this?" my tone trembled with uncertainty.

"This is Angel's place. She is the resident soothsayer."

Cole

"How can you choose her over the pack?"
"She isn't even one of us. Why protect her?"
"Is she even human anymore? Or is she a vampire?"
The pack descended, their words like fangs tearing into

me. Doubt, fear, anger—each accusation sank deeper, drawing blood and sapping my strength. I stood besieged, weathering the onslaught. No defense could shield me from the relentless attack. I bore the brunt, wounds gaping, resolve wavering. Still, the savage barrage continued, merciless, inescapable. But I could not yield or give them the satisfaction they sought. I steeled myself, roots firm despite the storm, and let the poison words run their course. I would endure, as I always had, hardened by these trials, carried forward by sheer will. This too shall pass. And when the pack retreated, I would remain, bloodied but unbroken, to continue the fight.

But are they wrong? Could I protect them if she turns out to be evil?

But she couldn't be, could she? No, it was inconceivable. Violet was no more a threat than I was a vicious monster. Though I stood tall and robust in my werewolf form, I posed no danger to my pack—I was their guardian, not their menace. I saw only goodness and fragility when I looked at Violet's gentle face. In my heart was the stirrings it had never had. No she-wolf had ever ensnared a fierce longing and focus of protection in me.

Yet after an hour enduring their ruthless barrage of accusations, I was left shaken. Though finally released from their scrutiny, doubts plagued my mind. I sought solace under the light of the moon, turning to her for guidance.

I entered the hallowed halls of the temple; it was a humbling experience, and I lowered myself to the ground before the resplendent golden altar. My heart was heavy with sorrow, and I allowed the bitter tears to stream from my eyes, unafraid of the vulnerability they revealed. It was a lesson my father had imparted to me before his mysterious death, the understanding that emotions were meant to be felt, whether they were ones of joy or despair. Emotions were simply a part of the human experience, neither good nor bad, but an essential aspect of our existence.

"Mother Moon, please hear me. I do not know which way to turn. I do not know what to do about Violet... or my heart," I implored, my voice trembling with uncertainty.

Listen to it, came the faint response carried on the gentle winds.

"It says nothing, Mother," I protested, my resolve strong. I refused to yield to my heart's tumultuous yearning, convinced it would lead me astray. I needed to rely on my head to make rational decisions for the pack's sake and the fragile peace that held them together.

Listen to it, the voice whispered once more, insistent and gentle.

I closed my eyes, still hesitant, but I couldn't ignore the silent plea any longer. Reluctantly, I allowed myself to listen, not to the voice of reason, but to the quiet stirrings of my heart. Violet's presence had disrupted our lives, but could I turn against her so easily?

"She would divide us. She is not one of us. I must think of the children," I argued.

Are the children not with their leader? Should their leader not love? the voice inquired, challenging my resolve.

"Love is a luxury I cannot afford, Goddess," I stated firmly, clinging to my duty as a shield against the complexities of my emotions.

You are a fool, the voice whispered. *You'd deny your heart and the Goddess herself.*

Frustration coursed through me, my tears blending with the earth beneath my hands. The Goddess herself had cast her judgment upon my uncertainty, revealing the depths of my inner turmoil. She saw me as torn, indecisive, and, in a way, weak. The weight of my responsibilities as Alpha bore on me like a heavy yoke, but her persistent voice urged me to listen, to confront the storm of emotions within my heart.

If I were to reject Violet, to dismiss her as my pack and my head demanded, it would feel like a betrayal of my soul. She was real, not just a distant fantasy but a living, breathing woman who had unlocked emotions I'd only dreamed of. The thought of her by my side, carrying our child and emanating love, stirred a fierce longing within me. Yet, I chastised myself for such reveries, labeling them delusions and illusions, a path I hesitated to tread.

"You know your father had the same dilemma," someone said.

I started and turned to look behind me. It was Magnus. He hobbled my way.

"With whom?"

"Why, your mother. She was from a rival faction, still were-wolf, but we were not as friendly as we are now. She'd fallen and hit her head. Yes, this reminds me of that specifically," he said.

"But there's more Magnus, she's...."

"She holds magical qualities, eh?" he said, stealing my breath away.

"How...."

"I told you, son, this very thing happened many years before you were born."

I frowned, sure he was mistaken. "But Magnus, mother has no power."

Magnus laughed. Then he chilled my bones when he leaned in and whispered, "Are you sure?"

CHAPTER 5

Awakenings

Cole

As the sun dipped below the trees, yielding the sky to the moon's luminous reign, Magnus's words haunted me. Their implications were almost surreal as if part of some strange vision or hallucination. I grappled for solid ground amidst revelations that were too mystifying to grasp. My mother, a sorceress––could it really be so? But Magnus's certainty rang true, however incomprehensible. What opaque history had spawned his shrouded knowledge?

"What do you mean to say, Magnus?" I asked.

"I've said it plain as day. Your mother knows magic, just as you know the hunt," Magnus said with a twinkle in his eyes.

"Mom knows..." I couldn't say it. This had to be a mistake. "But how?"

"I'm no soothsayer, boy. But she sat on her magic all these years, and the same flows through your blood. I kept the secret for my friend until you turned the age I thought you could handle it."

I got off my ass and stared off. Mom. Dad. Violet. How much farther does this go?

"Well, what are you going to do? Keep denying the Goddess' wishes? Come, son." Magnus beckoned me out of the hallowed halls.

"What can I do, Magnus? I have feelings for Violet, but how can it be when we've only just met?"

"Love is as shrouded in mystery as the Goddess herself. But your father fell hard as well. Lindy is quite beguiling, as is your lass."

I turned to view the older man in the moonlight. "Did you care for her?"

Magnus laughed but did not reply.

As we approached, thirty sturdy men stood with weapons. I frowned and tensed, but Rafe stepped out.

"Brother," Rafe's voice held a note of reason amidst the rowdy group's agitation. "I thought it best we continue the hunt as the festival is tomorrow, and our supply is still in the lower end. It might help calm the others."

He held my lance. I grabbed it and nodded to him.

"Or did we need to wait while you play footsie with your piece, *mighty leader*," came Rhys' voice.

I frowned. "You got something to say, Rhys?"

He sneered. "Oh no, just making sure you're able to perform your duties, or do we need to retire you?"

"No one is retiring me unless they want their ass handed to them. Come on, wolves, let's go."

I turned, the men close behind as we delved into the deep forest's heart. Moonlight filtered through ancient boughs, casting a silvery glow on the path ahead. I led with quiet resolve, our footfalls falling into steady rhythm amid the tranquil night.

Thoughts churned as we moved on in silence. My mother, magical? The notion was incomprehensible, with no hint of such power in my childhood. Yet Magnus insisted a formidable gift lay dormant within her, much like Violet's developing abilities. Had my father known the truth? Is that why they were drawn together--two mystical beings united? Questions swirled, but the hunt required focus. Answers would come in time.

Mother Moon's siren call resonated within, an irresistible summons to my wolf form. Her beckoning was a potent enticement, as seductive as a lover's tender words. My wild spirit had lain asleep for too long, buried under the mantle of leadership and its various burdens.

The wilderness, once my refuge, had faded to memory as duty kept me tethered. But longing swelled inside, a yearning for youth's unfettered days racing the pack across untamed plains and rolling hills. I could still recall those joyful moments baying playfully at the moon, surrendering wholly to the wild essence within.

Beneath the moonlight, Lumiharts roamed the forest depths, their graceful forms adding an ethereal aura to the undergrowth. Their lithe bodies shimmered as they stepped through the brush, fur-like tapestries woven from silvery starlight. Majestic, spiraled horns crowned their heads, catching the lunar glow with captivating radiance.

Venturing deeper into the ancient woods, my pack tracked the hypnotic creatures; senses heightened to each subtle sound. The Lumiharts' beauty was undeniable, but duty pressed heavily on my mind--my people depended on this hunt before the imminent festival. Predator and prey forged a timeless bond as the gentle moon embraced us all. I turned to the men behind me, my face serious.

"Fan out!" I ordered the wolves. "And keep silent. Our prey is near."

"I spotted some Hallobears," Alden whispered.

I nodded. "They will soon head south, fan out, and kill only what you can."

The others quickly dispersed, moving stealthily between the trees. Well, most of them. Rhys lingered, glaring and sneering as he often did.

"Think you're still fit to lead, Cole?" Rhys taunted. "Or are you too distracted by your pet human?"

I stiffened, biting back a harsh retort. Now was not the time to appear weak.

"Stay focused on the hunt," I replied. "We can settle disputes later."

Rhys scowled but said no more as he shifted into wolf form and loped off. I was grateful for the reprieve from his antagonism.

I hadn't been in my wolf form in a long while, and I ached for it. The liberty of being in my freest form was more appealing than cold water on the hottest day.

Just then, a twig snapped to my left. I whirled, a snarl on my lips, ready to take down the threat. Out of the corner of my eye, I glimpsed teeth, fur, and claws. A Hallobear had been stalking us, and now it was fixated on me. I wondered if I could shift, but a stirring was behind me.

My lance was gripped tight in my trembling hand, and I felt the impending attack of the Hallobear before it even happened. I locked eyes with the furious beast, a formidable foe equal in size and might and one whose malice burned fiercely in its gaze. Massive claws scraped the forest floor as it prepared to strike.

In a split-second, I raised my gleaming steel lance, the moonlight reflecting off its menacing point. The Hallobear lunged at me, all bared fangs and unrestrained aggression. I had to act fast. With deft agility, I dodged its ferocious advance, my chance escape missing the snap of its jaws. The creature reared on its hind legs, unleashing a mighty roar that echoed through the forest. I, too, raised my voice in a fierce battle cry and charged toward the Hallobear, my lance poised and ready to attack. But it was a dangerous dance. I was on guard when we circled each other, tension thick in the air.

As the beast lunged again, I steadied my breath and focused on my target. With lightning speed, I thrust the lance toward it. The silver-tipped weapon struck the Hallobear in its muscular shoulder. With an aggressive swipe, it sent the lance flying to the forest floor, far from my reach. Undeterred, we continued to battle.

We moved in tandem, locked in a death dance, our primal instincts taking over. I grappled with the beast, my hands shifting to keep its slashing claws away from my vulnerable flesh. The creature jerked and writhed, attempting to dislodge me and sink its lethal teeth into my neck. Every muscle in my body flexed as I wrestled with the mighty adversary. I pitched the Hallobear away from me in a surge of primal strength. Rolling to my feet, I swiftly retrieved my lance, knowing the battle was far from over.

"Time to end this!" I said.

Under the moonlight, I had an unobstructed view of my target. My grip on the lance was steady. I aimed and thrust it, the weapon finding its mark with a sickening squelch as it impaled the beast's chest. A roar of agony and fury rents the air, echoing through the forest. The creature staggered and fell, its life force fading rapidly. However, my victory was not without its cost. As the Hallobear collapsed, its massive claws found their mark on my exposed chest, leaving behind three ragged, searing gashes that ran from my nipple to my ribcage. I gritted my teeth against the scorching pain, the stench of my blood mixing with the overpowering musk of the fallen beast.

Quickly, I covered the wound with my hand, doing my best to staunch the bleeding. As I stood there, my chest heaving with the effort, my pack mates approached, each carrying their successful kills from the hunt. It was a hard-fought battle, but we had secured enough meat to feed our pack for the winter.

Gratitude swelled within me. Providing for my people, as did their skill and teamwork, filled me with pride. But satisfaction was tempered by the sting of the gashes now hidden beneath my vest. I would need treatment, but my pack mates need not worry. Morale remained high; no need to dampen it with tales of a minor injury. We had survived and would feast well, thanks to our combined efforts.

Violet

I followed Lindy into the mysterious soothsayer's hut, unsure what to expect. The interior was lit with candles, drying herbs, and charms dangled from the rafters. Thick smoke from a small fire wafted through the space, carrying an earthy, medicinal scent.

The older woman, Angel, sat hunched on the floor amidst various bones, crystals, and bowls of colored powders. Her wizened face studied me closely as we entered, her dark eyes peering from under a fraying shawl.

"Come, child, let me look at you," she rasped, beckoning me forward. I hesitated, then stepped closer. With surprising speed, she grabbed my hands, turning them palms up as she scrutinized my skin. I resisted the urge to pull away.

"Hmm, interesting," Angel murmured. "Much potential,

yet still slumbering." She lifted her gaze to mine. "But the blood moon rises soon, yes? Then we shall see what awakens."

A shiver ran through me. How could this stranger know so much about the changes I was experiencing? I glanced back at Lindy, who grinned.

"Sit, both of you," said Angel, releasing my hands. We lowered ourselves to the dusty floor as she collected various items from around the room. Soon, she wafted pungent smoke over me while chanting mystical words. I coughed and waved my hand to clear the haze.

"Your past and future are clouded, but the present is clear child," the old woman muttered. "Keep close to the wolf that guards you. Your fates are bound."

I sucked in a shocked breath. Cole? Did she speak of Cole? Before I could ask, Angel leaned forward, grasping my chin. "Beware the lure of darkness," she warned. Her eyes pierced my soul.

"The Vampire King?" I said without thought.

"Ah, he aims to make you his, in more ways than one. To control you is to control your power. More than these lands have seen. Once you awaken, so too did the darkness awaken."

"Darkness? Which darkness do you speak of, Angel?" Lindy asked, making me uncomfortable.

"All will be known in time. I do not wish to give all the answers. For what fun would that be? You should take care of your magic; it is time."

My eyes widened, and my head snapped to Cole's mother. "You have magic, too?"

"Aye, I do not remember all, but my mother practiced magic in secret. She was a wise woman like Angel, and she passed the gift to me."

"What can you do?"

"I can bring the rains when our lands have been barren. Basic elemental magic."

I turned to eye Angel. "How am I intertwined with Cole?"

The aged woman smiled. "The war between beast and man surely approaches. Peace has been broken long before this. The Goddess will share what she wishes. You are special to her: you and your beloved. You should return. He needs you."

"But I want to know more. There is so much I don't understand, can I please...."

"Enough! There is only so much one should learn when the Goddess deems it so. Can you not hear him?" Angel asked.

I blinked and listened.

Violet? Violet, where are you, love? Cole's baritone came into my head. *Come quickly. I am hurt.*

I stood and gasped.

Lindy stood, too. "What is it, Violet?"

"We must go. It was wonderful to meet you, Angel." I grabbed Lindy's hand and led her to the door. I turned back once.

"Yes, we will meet again. Go!" Angel responded.

I nodded, my heart swelling with gratitude. Lindy and I hurried back into the shadowy forest, retracing our steps down the winding path. Moonlight filtered through the canopy of trees, lighting our way as we returned to the outskirts of the Bloodmoon Compound.

Upon entering the camp, the atmosphere had shifted palpably from before. The uneasy tension hanging over the pack had vanished, replaced by an aura of vibrant excitement and lively eagerness.

Women and girls moved purposefully, adorning every inch of the grounds with vibrant banners and intricate decorations to prepare for the fast-approaching festival. The vivid colors and elaborate designs embellishing trees and structures created an enchanting scene. Over by a massive barbecue, the men of the pack gathered, their spirits visibly lifted after their successful hunt. Laughing voices and cheerful conversations mingled with the heavenly scents of roasting meat wafting through the celebratory air.

"It is wonderful, Lindy. We have enough food to carry us through the winter," Alden said with a broad, beaming smile, reflecting the collective joy that rippled through the group.

Another man, his wild brown hair reflecting the untamed spirit of the pack, stepped out from the gathering and warmly embraced Lindy. His hug concluded with a tender kiss on her cheek. "Mother Belinda, Cole has come through for us yet again," he exclaimed with genuine admiration and respect.

Lindy's eyes sparkled with a mixture of pride and longing. "Rafe, where is he? Where is my son?" she inquired with a heartwarming eagerness.

Rafe frowned. "He said he'd tired himself out. He went to lie down."

Lindy turned to me. I nodded.

Before I left, I grabbed her hand. "Mother Lindy, I won't let anything happen to him."

She smiled and kissed my hands, then my cheek.

I hurried to Cole's hut with fear in my heart. I opened the door to glimpse him lying on his side on his gigantic bed. I slid off my shoes at the doorway and padded to his side.

"Cole?"

He turned and eyed me, then grimaced.

I frowned. "You're hurt."

"Yes." He covered his chest where the vest clung to his skin. Upon closer look, it was wet, and a pungent metallic scent tinged the air. I waved his large hand away, which was damp, and pulled the vest aside. The claw marks looked angry and irritated.

"Should I get someone?" I asked.

"No, they'd only fuss. I just needed you to be here with me."

"I don't want to see you hurt," I murmured. My small

hand reached out, fingers tentative, hovering over the angry wound marring Cole's chest. The pain etched on his face was an agony to witness. A powerful urge surged within me—an ardent desire for his pain to vanish, for the wound to disappear at a mere thought.

I closed my eyes, screwing them tight as I summoned every ounce of concentration. I willed with fierce determination for him to heal, focusing wholly on this singular goal. In that charged moment, my fervent wish became a potent force. Cole cried out, startling me.

My eyes blinked open, alarmed that I may have unintentionally caused him harm. But astonishment swiftly replaced my fear. His chest was now unblemished, the skin smooth and unbroken where jagged gashes had just been. Though blood still dampened his vest, the wounds had miraculously disappeared. My awakening powers had responded, healing him in as my deepest desire. I marveled at their astonishing potential, unable to grasp what I could now achieve.

"You *are* a witch," came Cole's astonished voice.

I eyed him. "Do I displease you? Will you throw me out now?"

"Is that what you wish, love?" he asked, rising from lying prone.

"My wish is to remain with you," I whispered. I crawled to him slowly and straddled his lap. He frowned and caressed my cheek. I closed my eyes at his soft touch.

"You hope to remain here with me?" he asked.

I opened my eyes, "... as your mate." I whispered.

"It goes against our tradition. We mate and marry our own. We don't even usually marry other werewolves outside our sects. My father had much to make up for as the Bloodmoon Brotherhood almost kicked him out."

"Why didn't they?" I asked.

"He didn't get the chance to tell me. He died suddenly

before we continued our conversation, and I dare not ask my mother."

Tears sprung into my eyes as I leaned over him. I brought my nose to his neck and inhaled his strong, male scent. It activated a bevy of sensations below my waist. I'd never so much wanted a man to kiss me as I did then. Cole grabbed the back of my head. His eyes searched mine.

"Kiss me," I commanded.

"Be still, woman, you know not what you ask."

"Kiss me or leave me to die. Because if you do not, I will surely."

His thick lips met mine the next second, and electricity surged within me. It was the magic that passed between us, and I experienced a wealth of emotions, all of them delicious. I opened my mouth as his thick tongue entered it, and I moaned. I caressed his tongue with mine, and something hardened beneath me. Cole's arms wrapped me in their warm embrace, and between my thighs became wetter than memory afforded me to remember. I ran my fingers through his coarse black hair, and the kiss deepened. Cole's hand ran over my back, down it, and over my ass, which he caressed.

He flipped us so that he lay on top of me. Having his large, sturdy frame covering me felt so right. I knew then that we would make love, and I wanted it.

I brought my legs around Cole's waist, and a part of his pants hit me right in the middle of my body. I moaned as that deliciousness enveloped me. I moved my lower half against him. He brought his enormous hand to rest on my waist to stop me, and he kissed my neck. The hair on my nape stood, and I was melting. His large hand covered my silk-covered mound, and I licked my lips.

"Have you been with a man?" Cole asked. His baritone was even deeper.

"No."

He frowned. "I cannot take your virginity. Not in my state."

"What is your state?"

"It would be too rough," he whispered.

I stuck my nose in his neck again and inhaled. "I don't care. I want you. Make love to me, Cole. I am yours to have."

Feeling brave, my hands roamed his muscular body, from his large, almost bare chest to his waist to his pants. I ran my hand over the top of it and hurriedly unfastened them. He didn't stop me. His breathing accelerated. I stuck my hand into the uncharted territory and grabbed him. He was hard and thick. Cole moaned in my ear. I rubbed him, and he bit my neck. His hand that had tried to wrangle my bucking hips slid into my panties, and his thick fingers touched my center, exciting the magic in me.

Just as another lusty thought blasted through my head, a hurried knock came from the door. Cole rose, as did I. My heart thumped wildly for this man, and the absence of his physical body chilled my soul. I didn't want him to leave, not yet. He looked at me and smiled as though he could sense my displeasure.

"I will return, love." He kissed my forehead. I frowned, but it might have been a pout. Amusement danced in his eyes.

He ran a thumb over my lips. Then he climbed off me and got to his feet. He'd fastened his pants by the time he'd reached the door. My heartbeat thumped at every footfall. Who could it be at this late hour? What would they want? Would they call him away? I didn't know how much longer I could wait to have him.

Cole swung the door open, and his mother stood there looking spooked. My heart lurched.

"Mother, what troubles you?" Cole asked.

"Son, you must come quick. A voice has demanded your presence by name."

Cole furrowed his brows. "Voice?"

"Yes, she's demanded that you and Violet come to the square. I suggest you hurry."

"She?" I asked, joining Cole at the door.

"Yes. I believe it is... the Goddess."

CHAPTER 6
Prophecy Unveiled

Cole

My heart was winding up about to spin out of control. And why not? A supernatural presence had summoned Violet and me. I had no idea what to expect. My mother's nervous words still reverberating in my eardrums, bouncing in my head. My palms began to sweat and though the night was cool, so did my brow. Villagers rushed about, anxiety on their faces as they mirrored my expectation. What would happen when we entered the square?

Each step that took Violet and I closer caused my stomach to tighten. I looked at Violet to gauge her reaction. Her profile revealed little other than pale skin. But she kept her head high despite all that had happened.

We stood before the crowd, waiting. The tribe's members watched as the ethereal orb descended, its luminescent glow casting a mesmerizing sheen upon the gathering. The crowd fell into a hushed reverence, their collective breath held in anticipation. As the orb gently touched the stage, the glowing beams of moonlight radiated outward, bathing the surroundings in an otherworldly, silvery glow.

"Cole Wilderwolf, do you know who I am?" a loud, commanding female voice asked.

"Mother Moon?" I questioned.

As the luminous orb gently unfurled, it unveiled an awe-inspiring figure—a woman of otherworldly beauty. Her silver-white hair cascaded like a radiant waterfall down her back, shimmering with a radiance that mirrored the constellations in the night sky. Her skin exuded a warm, inviting brown hue reminiscent of the sweet chocolate often enjoyed by the pack's youngest members. Her eyes, as deep and mysterious as the cosmos, held a timeless wisdom and an innate kindness.

The gathered members, along with Violet and I, bowed our heads in unison to acknowledge the divine presence before us. The celestial aura surrounding the Goddess filled the square with a profound reverence.

"Rise, Bloodmoon Brotherhood," the Goddess spoke, her voice carrying the weight of the ages.

The villagers straightened themselves and gazed upon the resplendent deity. Her eyes first fell upon Violet, and a gentle smile graced her lips as if she had anticipated Violet's presence all along.

"Yes, you will suffice," the Goddess affirmed, then turned her attention to me. I bowed my head, demonstrating my respect. The Goddess continued, "Cole Wilderwolf, your heart is torn by conflicting emotions. Do you dare deny my will to my face?"

I bowed my head again, acknowledging my inner turmoil. "I have no desire to offend you, milady."

"Will you heed the call of your heart?" she inquired.

I gazed upon her, and my eyes briefly met the curious gazes

of the villagers. Magnus showed approval in his eyes, Rafe viewed in wonder, and Rhys appeared deep in contemplation. The gravity of my decision was palpable.

"I do not wish to displease you, milady. My conflict is with my position. I have led my people with all that I am and have. I listen to the people and try to feel what they do. If you have willed it, milady, I will not turn away from my duty."

"Long ago, I set the wheels in motion that you would be Alpha one day for this very time."

I frowned, not understanding. It was on the tip of my tongue to ask, but I didn't.

"Do you wish to reject Violet?" the Goddess asked. Beside me, Violet gasped.

I turned to face her, fear evident in her beautiful eyes. The fear that I would cast her aside, the fear that I would desert her. It tugged at my heart.

The Goddess's declaration had brought us to a pivotal moment, one I couldn't ignore. Not anymore.

"No, Goddess. I accept her. I have felt drawn to her since we first met." I declared, my voice steady and unwavering.

The Goddess responded with a warm smile. "It is as it should be. Now, do you wish to take Violet as your mate?"

I let out a sigh, my gaze never leaving Violet. "Yes, milady. It is my heartfelt wish."

The villagers reacted with mixed emotions, stirring a murmur that swept through the crowd, ranging from anger to bewilderment. Camille looked at me with disbelief, and Rhys wore a frown.

The Goddess raised her hand, and the residents fell silent. "Hush, my children. These two are destined lovers, their union written in the stars before their births, long before any of you arrived. Traditions must evolve with the times. The era of peace will end soon, and you will need your leader and his mate. You will seal your fates if you cast them out of your hearts. Heed my warning, for I have spoken."

The Goddess turned her gaze back to us, her smile filled with warmth. "This union is blessed and shall remain so for all eternity."

A voice from the crowd said, "What of the vampires? Will they initiate a war?"

The Goddess turned to address the villagers once more. "Bloodmoon Brotherhood, the war between the factions was decided long before. Even I cannot maintain peace, but there will be one who will bridge the divide. One who will ease the impending nightmare. There will be respite."

A trembling voice from a woman in the crowd asked, "Goddess, who will bring us peace? Who will secure it during the looming war?"

Instead of answering, the Goddess turned her gaze to Violet and me. "Violet Belladonna, you will seek answers, and answers you shall find. You must embark on a quest to retrieve a memory crystal."

Murmurs filled the air as the villagers grappled with the revelation.

"I task you, Cole Wilderwolf, to accompany Violet on her expedition."

"But who will take care of us while you are gone?" Agnus asked.

"Be still. Have I not provided for you and kept you safe all this time?" the Goddess asked. Thunder rumbled ominously, and lightning streaked across the night sky, leaving everyone awestruck.

Agnus, humbled by the display of divine might, bowed. "Forgive me, Goddess."

The Goddess, her presence an enigma of power and grace, accepted Agnus's apology. "Cole will appoint a warrior to oversee your safety, and I shall be by his side. You need not fear the intrusion of other factions in your absence, for I have decreed it."

As the Goddess's gaze turned to me, our path became clear. With determination, I made my choice. "I appoint Rafe to take my place as leader while I accompany Violet on her quest."

The Goddess nodded, her ethereal form gradually fading into a shimmering ball of light. Her words resonated in the air, a promise of leadership and protection. "Fear not, Cole, for I shall be with you."

The Goddess's blessing had set our journey into motion, and I couldn't deny the sense of destiny that enveloped Violet and me. She turned to me and hugged me. I hugged her back, hit by the full gravity of what had just transpired. I'd never sleep tonight. I could only feel the moon's pull on my wolf form, the yearning for Violet in my loins, not to mention the adrenaline rush in my veins from knowing that I would accompany Violet on a pursuit of her memories.

What is her role in this life?

So much more now that I'd declared in front of everyone that she'd be my mate. I sighed and squeezed Violet a little tighter.

Violet

The early morning brought a gentle mist that enveloped the riverside, casting a mystical aura over the scene. The village was still abuzz with excitement from the visitation of the Goddess, whispers flowing like the river's current. The young women gathered, their laughter and camaraderie infectious. They took me under their wing, leading me to the riverbank as they explained the preparations for the night's festivities. Their collective expressions and actions were inviting and inclusive, though I was awkward.

The icy river water greeted my naked skin. Nudity was an accepted part of their rituals, and I tried my best not to let my cheeks burn with embarrassment. I averted my gaze, but the temptation of curious glances was everywhere.

"You must be quite special," a girl whispered in my ear, her voice tinged with a playful tone. I met the gaze of a short girl with dark hair and captivating eyes. She sported a mischievous smirk that hinted at secrets hidden beneath the surface. "My name is Camille. I've never seen Cole so determined," she remarked as if she could read my thoughts.

I managed a timid smile, unsure how to respond to her observation. Camille quickly shared a bottle with me, and as I accepted it, the scent of the wild swirled around me. It was an enchanting mixture of fragrances that held a promise. "Use this to wash your hair and body. It's said to draw your lover to you and ignite their passion. They'll be in a fury of desire with the moon's pull tonight. It guarantees a night of unforgettable lovemaking."

I poured some of the fragrant mixture into my palms and began to apply it to my hair, its tingling sensation awakening my senses. Camille offered to help rinse it out. I washed my body as well. As we dressed, the other women departed with a shared enthusiasm for the night to come.

In my excitement, I had forgotten my shoes and turned to retrieve them before rejoining the others. Camille offered to accompany me, but I insisted she go ahead without me. I hurried back to the riverside, the rushing water still echoing in my ears.

As I approached, I heard two men engaged in a heated argument. One voice sounded oddly familiar, drawing me closer to eavesdrop on their conversation.

"...do not double-cross me, mutt! I am taking a significant risk with you!" the first man's voice was tinged with anger.

"Now, now. Name-calling won't get us anywhere. I've provided you with everything you need. Now, hand over my payment!" the second man responded. His voice was familiar.

"Are you certain we can proceed tonight?" the first man inquired, doubt lacing his words.

"Of course. I am on duty. Besides, with everyone preoccupied by lust, security will be the last thing on their minds," the second man assured him.

"Remember your place. You wolves should focus less on breeding while the tide is in your favor," the first man retorted.

"Yeah, right. Just give me my money," the second man insisted.

I was intrigued yet uneasy, but I couldn't turn away. The men exchanged a bag and a parchment, speaking in hushed tones. A snapping twig beneath my foot drew their attention, and both men in shrouded attire turned to scan the area. Panic coursed through me as I recognized the man holding the money bag. I retreated, sprinting away from the scene until I collided with Camille, breathless and shaken.

"What happened, Violet?" Camille inquired with concern.

I hesitated, catching my breath, before I uttered, "I overheard something... something..."

"Ladies!" came the second man's voice right behind me. I swallowed and turned to face Rhys.

He smirked.

"What are you doing out here, Rhys? Spying?" Camille asked.

Rhys laughed. "Why spy when I can get the real thing for free?" His dark eyes landed on me. "How are you, Violet?"

"We have to go," I said. Camille thankfully grabbed my hand and led me away. I'd never been so frightened by anyone in my life. I didn't know what he was up to, but I was sure it had to do with Cole.

"Where is Cole?" I asked as we stepped foot back into the camp.

"He's probably helping with the barbecue. Why?"

"I have to talk to him."

"Later. We must get you ready."

I frowned. "We?"

Lindy opened the door to her hut next to Cole's, smiling. "We must prepare you for the festival, my dear."

Many hours later....

Butterflies were in my belly as I proceeded down the aisle... The groom was shrouded in shadows, his back to me.

I was so happy to marry Cole, so delighted we'd be having such a ceremony.

I turned to all of them: Camille, Rafe, Magnus, Lindy...

They all smiled.

"Do you take this man to be yours?" the official asked.

"I do," I squeaked happily.

"Do you take Violet as your bride?"

Cole turned slowly, and when he turned to me, my eyes widened in horror.

It was not Cole but a pale-faced man with dark, cold brown eyes.

"I do," he said.

Gasping, I jolted upright, my chest heaving with the remnants of the dream that had stirred my heart to a frenzied rhythm. The village women had spent the morning painting intricate designs on my arms and legs to prepare for the upcoming festival. Afterward, they'd styled our hair, with Lindy taking charge of mine. Her smile was radiant as she worked. She donned a white dress that reversed the effects of time, making her appear decades younger.

"Did you hear me? I said the festival is starting. Hurry!" Lindy's voice broke through my momentary reverie. I blinked, gazing up at her cheerful appearance, embodying the festivities.

"Of course," I replied, rising to my feet. I ran my fingers along the silk dress that Lindy herself had spun for me. The fabric clung to my body. I contemplated the night ahead and all the magical moments already behind us.

Lindy reached out, her warm hand enveloping mine, and as the rush of anticipation coursed through my veins, her latent magic mingled with mine. She squeezed my hand, a sudden arc of electricity crackling between us. Giggling, we raced towards the square, where the festivities were already in full swing.

Other maidens darted around us, young men with bare chests pursuing them in spirited chases. Couples were scattered throughout the square, locked in passionate kisses beneath the radiant glow of the full moon. The scent of seared meat, sweet wine, and fresh vegetables hung in the air, carried on the gentle winds that whispered through the village.

I scanned the jubilant crowd for Rhys but couldn't spot him amid the festive throng. Our mad dash ended as we approached the head of a group of long tables adorned with a sumptuous spread of food, an array of wine bottles, and bowls brimming with delectable offerings.

Lindy tapped a burly man on the shoulder, and a strange sense of déjà vu washed over me. I nearly recoiled, but my anxiety eased when Cole turned to face me, a mug in his hand. Like the other men present, he wore pants but no shirt, displaying his formidable, muscular chest. He was twice as imposing as the other men, and I couldn't help but admire his presence. His eyes roved from my hair to my bare feet, and he opened his mouth as if about to speak. But I remembered what I had witnessed earlier in the day.

"Cole, I must speak with you," I blurted, a sense of urgency in my voice.

"What's troubling you, Violet?" Rhys's voice suddenly emerged from behind me, sending a dark cloud of uncertainty over me. Whether I desired it or not, this festival would mark a turning point in my life.

CHAPTER 7

Moonlit Union

Violet

A storm brewed in Cole's intense gaze despite the vibrant festival as he eyed me. It was as though he sensed a discourse within me. As others continued to chat and drink, I also noticed their gaze fixed on me.

"Violet," Rhys said again, "What troubles you?"

I hesitated for a moment. "It was nothing. I just thought I saw something in the shadows."

"Ah! Imbibing will do that to you," Rhys said with a knowing smile. He held a cup, too.

Does he mean to celebrate my love's downfall?

"Violet, are you sure you are alright?" Cole asked.

"Yes, I am fine."

He graciously pulled my seat out, and I sat with my hands in my lap. Rhys's intense stare bore into me, leaving a lingering sensation. Cole excused himself momentarily and gathered a group of men, one of whom was the insufferable Rhys. I caught the phrase "increased security." My heart sank, knowing unexpected dangers might taint our perfect night.

"You look beautiful," a deep, male voice complimented me from behind. I turned to find Rafe standing there, transformed for the festival. His usually untamed curls were now neatly combed, and he wore an unfamiliar warmth in his smile.

"Thank you," I replied, a note of concern tingeing my voice.

"Something wrong?" Rafe inquired, his thoughtful eyes locked onto mine.

I leaned in and whispered, "I saw Rhys in the woods, talking to someone."

"Who?" Rafe asked.

"I didn't see the other person. The man called Rhys a mutt, and they exchanged things. He gave Rhys a bag of money, and Rhys handed over a parchment."

Rafe's brows furrowed. "I take it you didn't tell Cole?"

"I didn't have the chance. Rhys keeps appearing, and I fear something may happen to Cole," I confessed, my eyes widening with worry.

Rafe's expression. "Not on my watch."

With that, he hurried over to where Cole stood among other villagers, engaging in conversation and laughter. Rafe whispered something in Cole's ear, prompting the men to take off hastily.

"Have some wine," a cheerful voice offered as I turned. It was Camille, pouring me a glass.

I accepted it with gratitude, a warm smile gracing my lips. "Just what I need." The sweet and fragrant liquid filled the glass, and with little thought, I took a hearty gulp. The wine's rich flavor and aroma ignited something in my brain, and its effects were immediate.

"Be careful," Camille cautioned as she explained, "They

make it strong for the festival. Our vineyard is available year-round, but this is an older brand, reserved for celebrations."

A spirited young man approached Camille and kissed her cheek warmly. "Save a dance for me, lovely Camille," he requested, a playful glint in his eye.

Camille giggled in response, and he grabbed her, tickling her playfully until her laughter filled the air. "Stop it, you fool, or you'll make me spill my wine," she teased.

With a howl, he raced off like a whirlwind to join the other men piling broken wood into a fire pit. The wood was set ablaze with expert precision, and the flames shot up tall as if by some magical force.

In response, I closed my eyes and focused on my magical abilities, seeking to calm the fire and my racing heart. As I opened my eyes, I witnessed a peaceful and controlled bonfire, demonstrating my focus's effectiveness.

"Miss me?"

My gaze shifted upward to find Cole's familiar face adorned with a reassuring smile. He leaned in and kissed my cheek; his presence warmed me.

"What are you wearing?" he asked, catching me off guard.

I frowned and looked at my dress, thinking he didn't like it. "What do you mean?"

"Forgive me. I only meant your scent is different tonight. What is it?"

I smirked. "Something to tempt you. Is it working?"

He grinned, and my lust for him increased. "Oh yes!"

I giggled, but I remembered that bastard Rhys. "Is everything alright?"

"It is now," he replied, a glint of confidence in his eyes.

Cole cleared his throat. As if by an unspoken command, the bustling crowd settled, their animated conversations coming to a halt. They reached for their cups one by one, each sporting welcoming smiles. The atmosphere had lifted, becoming more joyful, and I marveled at the transformation.

"By the way, you look... enchanting," Cole whispered in my ear.

My cheeks warmed.

A pair of young men approached the gathering, burdened by a large steel vat. Two additional men quickly moved forward to help, and as a team, they gently placed the weighty container onto the wooden table. The vat's deep crimson liquid contents caught my attention and widened my eyes. The air was filled with anticipation, making it clear that this liquid played a crucial role in the celebration. Before long, the crowd passed around mugs, and people eagerly started pouring the mysterious red mixture. Cole filled mugs for both of us, filling me with curiosity.

"Mother, will you say the blessing."

Lindy stood, grinning ear to ear, and then she blew her son a kiss. "Under the light of the sacred moon, we gather as one, united in heart and spirit. May the Goddess's blessings envelop us, protecting our land and strengthening our bonds. May our love and unity shine as brightly as the moon above. The ties bind us together by loyalty, trust, and magic on this night. Let the Goddess's grace guide our path and fill our hearts with joy and prosperity. Blessed be."

"Blessed be!" The joyful chorus of voices rose from the crowd, and I joined in, raising my cup to my lips. A peculiar sensation took hold as I savored the semi-sweet notes of the festival's unique concoction. It started as a subtle tingling in my toes, a feeling that soon raced through my veins, setting my entire body alight with a thrilling energy. My stomach somer-saulted with excitement and nervous anticipation, and I couldn't help but lick my lips in response.

"Let's eat!" Cole declared, and the jubilant crowd helped themselves to plates brimming with various delicious dishes, each cooked and seasoned to perfection. With Cole taking charge, he expertly sliced up a wild boar, serving mouthwatering portions to all who gathered.

People savored their meals, praising the barbecue and the head chef. In every direction, villagers engaged in lively conversations about the harvest and sought Cole's advice on various minor concerns. He responded with carefully considered answers, and I admired his intelligence and respectful approach to addressing issues without belittling others. I didn't know exactly what an Alpha was or did, but I saw him as an outstanding leader, and I was sure when the time came for war, it would be better in his hands than any other I'd met in the village.

Yet, as I savored the flavors of the feast, a shadow of unease passed over me. I furrowed my brows, attempting to recollect something that felt just out of reach. In the deepest corners of my mind, a distant memory emerged. A tall, grey-haired gentleman with a stern countenance who appeared robust came to mind.

A disconcerting impression accompanied this vague memory, which starkly contrasted with the festive revelry unfolding around me. I recalled overhearing two men as they talked about me, as though I were nothing more than a commodity they were negotiating.

"You'll have to break her in. She's an uptight bitch. Thinks too much of herself," my father had commented.

"I know just what to do with her," the other man, the same one from my dream, replied.

"You know, King Lysander, you have all you could want. Why do you want, Violet?"

"Your daughter is the possessor of magic. A potent kind."

"Magic, eh? You are messing with the wrong thing. Take in a bitch for the bedroom, not for being a freak."

A shudder ran through me as the memory played out, and

I couldn't help but wince. Yes, now I placed that freak, King Lysander, how I hated him and my father. They could both rot in Hell.

"Violet, are you alright, love?" Cole's caring voice snapped me back to the present.

I gazed at him, and a warm smile graced my lips. "Yes, Cole. Just a few unpleasant memories resurfacing."

"You're getting your memories back?"

"A little."

"Who——?"

"Come on, love birds. Now we dance!" Camille declared, her laughter ringing out as the same boy who had tickled her earlier snuck up and gave her another. Camile turned and tickled him in return. They ran off together, laughing.

Cole and I joined in the laughter. Our eyes locked, and Cole sprang up, extending his hand toward me. I accepted it with a smile, allowing him to guide me to the open space by the bonfire, where the younger couples swayed and twirled to the lively melodies played by the musicians.

Under the starlit sky, Cole led the dance, twirling me around with grace and rhythm, and the wind played with my hair as I laughed. The world faded away, leaving only the music and the exhilaration of being in Cole's arms. We danced to the next tune, but I couldn't help but notice that some mischievous youngsters had snuck away, their giggles dissipating into the night. I wondered what adventure they were embarking on.

"Cole? Where are they off to?" I caressed his smooth cheek.

"Would you like to see?" he asked.

I nodded. And he grabbed my hand, taking me into the woods.

Cole

My soul surged with purpose as I led Violet deeper into the heart of the forest. The moon hung high in the night sky, casting its silver glow upon our path. The distant sounds of celebration echoed around us, the joyous laughter and the melodies of lovers hidden among the trees. It was a night of secrets, shared desires, and the transformative power of the moon.

As we ventured further into the woods, the first howl of a transformation pierced the air. It was a reminder of the impending change, a primal call to the creatures of the night. I was both eager and apprehensive about my transformation. Would Violet, who had only just been introduced to our world, be repulsed by my change? Would she flee from me in fear or disgust?

But I couldn't allow such doubts to cloud my mind. I had to show her, to share this part of my life with her. It was why I was leading her to my favorite secret spot, where the moon's magic was potent. There, under the silver light, I hoped to reveal the true nature of my existence and the bond that connected us in this enchanted world.

"Where are we going, Cole?" Violet asked, and she giggled. It was music to my ears.

"Somewhere special, love. Patience."

"Mmm. And what will we do there?" she teased, squeezing my hand.

"Just you wait, my little Vivee," I said.

She giggled in response, and I grinned. Around us more movement and giggling. Then, moans and howls. Tonight, a lot of pups would come into being. But suddenly, I couldn't think of much more because Violet gasped. I glanced up to view the large waterfall.

The moonlight bathed it, transforming the cascading waters into a silvery curtain of enchantment. The sight was captivating, but my attention was drawn back to Violet, who stood beside me. Her eyes shimmered with a reflection of the moon's radiance, and I couldn't help but be captivated by her beauty in this magical moment.

I whispered, "It's like something out of a dream, isn't it, Vivee?"

"Yes," she whispered back. She eyed me, and her pupils dilated. I brought my lips to her soft ones, and a moan slipped from her. She grabbed the back of my head as I bent to scoop her into my arms. The scent of her body and hair was driving me insane. And yet, the pull into my wolf form called to me even more. I would change soon, and I wanted it. I set her on her feet.

I stumbled back, my breaths now quick and labored through my nose. The world shifted as my sense of smell intensified, overpowering me with each breath.

My brows raised as my hands lengthened, becoming paws, and my fingers grew razor-sharp claws. Breathing shifted to a primal rhythm, and the profound internal changes taking place to accommodate my impending wolf form made an impression on me. Falling to my knees, I gritted my teeth as bones snapped and realigned, forming hind legs in the place of my human limbs. The transformation continued as fur sprouted through my skin's pores, a shiver of pain accompanying each strand. The most agonizing part began when my ears elongated and sharpened, my nose and mouth extending into a lengthened snout filled with newly formed, sharp teeth. As the last piece of the puzzle, my vision underwent a dramatic shift.

Finally, with the transformation complete, I let out a howl to the moon, my cry echoing through the night. In my lupine form, I was aware of my imposing presence, with my light and dark gray fur and hulking size, yet Violet didn't shy away.

I'd almost forgotten she was with me. My large, wolfish head turned towards her, and she tilted her head with curiosity shining in her eyes.

"Does it hurt?" she whispered, her concern touching me.

I shook my head slightly. *No, not anymore.*

Oh, you can still do that? Violet's voice rang clear in my mind, and her surprise was evident.

If I could have widened my eyes, I would've, but I was a wolf now, and all I could do was focus on our connection. I answered her mentally. *I am not doing this; you are.*

Violet giggled softly in response.

Since when has this been happening? I inquired, my curiosity piqued.

"Since you were hurt," she replied. "You spoke in my head."

Get on my back, I offered, lowering and nuzzling her gently.

Violet climbed on, her fingers grasping my fur with a delicate touch.

Hold on! I instructed.

I reared up on my powerful hind legs with Violet securely on my back. She laughed joyously, the sound filling the night air, a sweet melody of pure delight. I raced off, gracefully navigating through the ancient trees with breathtaking speed. Violet whooped in the wind, her exhilaration becoming a contagious force that spurred me on. My powerful legs carried us effortlessly over babbling rivers, my immense size and strength making each leap look like child's play. We ventured deep into the wild, leaving the camp far behind, our spirits soaring under the moon's watchful eye.

With grace and power, we ascended a medium-sized mountain and found ourselves overlooking the sprawling expanse of Evernite. Villages and towns dotted the landscape, their lights shimmering like distant stars beneath the gentle moonlight. More rivers meandered through the terrain while other mountains rose majestically in the distance. As Violet shivered in the cool night air, she snuggled closer into my warm fur, her soft lips brushing against the back of my head as a whispered promise of trust and companionship.

"Show me more, Wolfie," she husked, her words igniting a fire within me.

I descended the mountain and met up with more of the pack. We ran together, our powerful forms moving in harmony. Some wolves had maidens in their human forms on their backs while other females raced with us. Their fur was lighter than the males', a blend of silver and gray, and together, we became a breathtaking symphony of fur, speed, and moonlit grace.

We all broke off on our paths, and I returned to the waterfall. Racing through the forest, I reached the serene crater where the cascade poured its refreshing waters. With an exhilarating leap, I soared and splashed into the cool, crystal-clear liquid. Violet shrieked in delight, her joy contagious. I surfaced, shaking off droplets, and she emerged as well, her laughter mingling with the symphony of nature's sounds.

She dipped under for a worrying amount of time. When she resurfaced, she held her gown above her head and threw it to the forest near the edge. She smiled.

"Change back, Wolfie. I want to make love," she whispered.

I dove under the water's surface. The shift began within

me, the power of transformation ebbing away. My body trembled momentarily, and I slowly began morphing into my human form. My strong, Alpha wolf form gradually gave way to my human self. Bones snapped, and skin rippled as the metamorphose continued. My fur receded, revealing tanned skin, and my limbs reshaped into human arms and legs.

A shiver ran through me as I treaded the waters. I swam up from the bottom and looked about. Violet awaited me with implied hunger. I swam to her and crushed her naked body against my own. Her legs wrapped around my waist as I treaded water for both of us. With my hands on her tiny, round ass, I slid my tongue into her warm, welcoming mouth. We stayed fused, our tongues intertwining and caressing. When I couldn't breathe, I broke away and kissed her long, elegant neck.

"I want you, Cole. Make me yours," she whispered.

I wrapped my arm around her waist while she clung to me. I swam until we reached the edge. Climbing out, I turned, and she held up her arms. I grabbed them and easily extracted her from the rippling water.

She smirked and lay on the forest floor. I stretched out over her, covering her nudity with my own. I trailed my kisses from her neck to her delicate clavicle and finally to her lovely breasts.

I took my time caressing their unique shape. Her dark pink nipples hardened as I licked them; I loved the feel of them on my tongue. Violet squirmed. I licked her areolas until she moaned deeply. She grabbed my head, holding me there. As I kissed her breasts, my other hand smoothed over her flat belly to her mound. I pushed her leg up to bend it and ran my fingertips over her center. She moaned again and began sucking my earlobe. I hardened a long while ago but, in my state, I would hurt her. I had to get her to my level.

I plunged a finger into her, and she squirmed. I frowned. "Does it hurt, love?"

"It's weird," she whispered.

I licked her neck and breathed heavily in her ear. "Mmm. Weird good or weird bad?"

"It's delicious. More. Give me more," she husked.

"Don't get greedy," I said with a chuckle.

"You make it all feel wonderful, my love," she said with a swat to my naked ass.

"Hey! Watch it!" We chuckled together.

I gently entered her opening with my two fingers; it was getting slippery. She was almost ready. I kissed her sweet neck again. That fragrance that had lured me to her once upon a time was strong, mingling with yet another scent. I licked her belly as she giggled and tousled my hair. All the while, my fingers slid in and out of her. I raised her leg and kissed her inner thigh.

"Mmm. Cole," she murmured.

"Yes, love?"

"Are you as big as your fingers?"

I stuck three fingers in her. "More like that."

"Oh my," she whispered and moaned.

I sat up and looked at her. The moonlight danced in her heated gaze. She slowly licked her lips. I grabbed my dick and circled it around her opening. She began breathing from her mouth. Her delicate hands grazed my chest, snaring my senses in a drunken dance of lust. She caressed my hips. I bent closer and slowly inched into her. She gripped my shoulders.

"Oh God!" she cried.

"Does it hurt, love?" I whispered again.

"All the way. Go all the way in!"

As maddening as it was, I didn't drive into her as my loins urged me to do. I slowly, inch by inch, expanded her until I was most of the way in. She gripped me so tightly that I responded with a groan. She was wet enough for me to slide easily into her. I began moving my hips slowly.

"Oh God, yes!" she cried, scratching my back.

I couldn't help it; there's only so much a man could endure. "Vivee, I'm going to go a little faster."

"Yes! Yes! Faster."

Her throaty moans were driving me to the brink, and I increased my speed. Her feet were aiding my intrusion into her, and I breathed heavily. She grabbed my hair.

"Dammit, Cole, fuck me!" she cried.

I lost it then. I began driving into her, losing my grip on reality and time itself. She was a warm welcome embrace, and I had to come, or my loins would detonate on their own. I straightened her legs and fucked her while she cried out passionately.

"Yes! Dear God! Yes! Oh my God!" she cried and stiffened. Her whole body seized, including her already tight opening. I couldn't hold back any longer, and I exploded within her. She jerked and moaned. I collapsed atop her, my breathing ragged.

"I'm sorry. I lost control."

"No. It was wonderful," she whispered and kissed my head. She stretched. "We should return to your hut for more."

I lifted my head, and my eyes met hers. "More?"

"Oh yes!" she whispered and kissed me.

As we made our way back to the camp, fingers intertwined, the world took on a surreal quality in the soft, silvery light of the moon. The night was alive with the enchanting melodies of singing insects, harmonizing with nature's orchestra. A contented sigh escaped my lips, and for a moment, the world held a quiet perfection.

Without warning, the tranquility shattered like glass. A rush of frenzied activity surrounded us as gleaming eyes pierced the inky blackness. Figures clad in shadowy black closed in from all directions, their movements swift and coordinated. Violet's terrified shriek pierced the night as she was abruptly torn from my grasp.

They'd outnumbered us, but my heart refused to surrender. I braced for action, but before I could react, a powerful blow to the head sent me spiraling into darkness, the last thing I saw being the terror etched on Violet's face.

CHAPTER 8
A New Alliance

<u>King Lysander</u>

awn's muted light filtered into the room as I was gripped by an ancient restlessness. Having forgone sleep and drunk the altered fae's blood, a potent elixir invigorating my veins with caffeinated magic, the air hummed with electric anticipation.

Shadows clung stubbornly to the edges of the encroaching morning, unwilling to relinquish their hold on the sunlight. Time was scarce, and I couldn't afford patience. My instructions had been explicit––the creature's mark must be erased from Violet's being. She was to be cleansed and dressed for her new station.

Perched at the edge of my bed, surrounded by an arrangement of instruments, I drummed my fingers to the urgent rhythm within. The room throbbed with quiet expectation as I awaited Violet's imminent arrival. The air crackled with escalating tension.

"Calm yourself, Master," Seraphina said.

My eyes feasted on the woman seated beside me. She had on a black lace push-up bra cradling large full breasts, accompanied by delicate black lacy panties that hinted at a clandestine sensuality. The black garter belt embraced her hips, securing the sultry promise of thigh highs, their obsidian sheen a captivating contrast against her porcelain skin. Completing the outfit were shiny black high heels.

A mysterious aura enveloped her as a black mask concealed her eyes, leaving only the intrigue of eagerness in its wake. Her hands, encased in black lacy gloves, holding a power of their own. Together, the ensemble formed a symphony of desire and mystery.

Her provocative gaze held mine, a silent challenge etched into the tilt of her head and a teasing flicker as she licked her lips. However, before the charged moment could unfold further, the door swung open with purpose, and my guards ushered in the captive Violet.

She was bound, a vision in a plum-colored cage dress adorned with numerous straps over the bodice. The dress featured daring slits that climbed up to the waist, revealing the allure of purple bikini-style panties beneath. Barefoot and defiant, Violet's wrists and ankles were secured to what appeared as a rigid board, yet in actuality it was a soft but firm support against which her back lay. A shiver of hatred, vivid and palpable, burned in her enchanting eyes despite the mouth covering that muffled any potential verbal rebellion.

The guards departed, abandoning us to our fun as they shut the door behind them.

Without being told, Seraphina rose with a queen's grace, sauntered to her own wall with a hook I'd constructed into it, and awaited me. I shackled her wrists and ankles to the wall in the shape of an X. I strolled to my bed, retrieved the shiny black whip, and looked at Violet. Her eyes riveted on the sexual weapon.

"You see, my dear, you will learn your place! Seraphina knows what's expected of her." I said and grabbed Seraphina's breasts. Seraphina giggled and moaned. I lowered the stiff cup and sucked on one of her hardened pink nipples. My eyes drifted to Violet's face. Much to my frustration, her eyes were closed.

I frowned and yelled. "Open your eyes, or I will hunt down that dog and kill him in front of you!"

In an instant, her eyes popped open, and she looked uncertain. Her hands balled into fists, and I anticipated her actions before she'd complete them. I smirked. "Oh no, Violet."

I strode forward and withdrew a substantial necklace from my robe. The chain was thick and interlocking, with a large yellow stone pendant. With a calculated motion, I placed it around her slender neck. She recoiled at my touch, but it mattered little. She would learn.

The mystical enchantment embedded in the necklace, intricately tied to the essence of vampire power, held steadfast against Violet's futile attempts to break free. The room crackled with an otherworldly energy.

"This medallion negates your power. Now, pay heed to what awaits you, or suffer the consequences, or let that mutt bear the burden," I declared, a grin stretching across my face. The spark of defiance in her eyes flickered and died, replaced by a resignation that quickened my undead heart. A triumphant laughter escaped my lips, echoing through the room.

Standing tall, I cracked the whip through the air with a sharp snap. Both Violet and Seraphina started, the sound reverberating through the room like a warning. Sensing the tension, I reveled in the charged atmosphere.

With a swift and deliberate motion, I flicked the whip

across Seraphina's milky white thighs. The crack resounded as the leather met her skin, leaving an angry red mark in its wake. A sly satisfaction danced in my eyes, relishing the visible consequence of Violet's disobedience.

"You think this is about sex? I say this is about power. He who wields the whip, wields the power. In my castle, the rule is to obey my EVERY command! I don't care if I tell you to kill your own family. You will do it and do it right!" I said.

"Ooh my liege, more!" Seraphina cooed.

"As you wish!" I said, my dick stiffening even further. I lashed the whip repeatedly, skillfully guiding it across Seraphina's form. The whip's dance left behind a mosaic of red marks on her skin; each strike a deliberate act in the intricate choreography of dominance and submission where the boundaries blurred.

As I ceased, my chest heaved with the exertion. Seraphina panted with both defiance and hunger. I smirked as I unchained her. She blew me a kiss. Then I turned to the other.

I approached Violet with a measured stride. With a swift motion, I tore the cloth from her mouth, revealing a mixture of terror and disdain in her eyes.

"Now, are you ready for me?" I taunted, a smug grin playing on my lips, fully aware of the response that awaited.

"You are the most revolting, demented, and utterly maddening thing I have ever met!" Violet's shriek of defiance cut through the air, a proclamation of loyalty that clashed with my will. Her words, hung in the air, creating a tension that hinted at a sense of impending reckoning. She hadn't declared her love for the mutt, but she might as well have. I rolled my eyes.

Rue the day I'd let her freely roam my castle! I should have chained her the day I bought her. Bought? How hilarious. How can you purchase something from someone that was never theirs in the first place?

"You damnable woman! That dog isn't fit enough for a woman of your caliber! He is a dog. A flea-ridden animal, do you not know of your power!" I said, flabbergasted.

"I don't care about my power. I don't care about yours. You have a woman, leave me be!" she shouted.

I took a moment to ponder the situation. This was new. Yes, she was disgusted as before, but this disgust differed from the day she escaped. I considered keeping this to myself. However, the temptation for mischief was too alluring. I would play Devil's Advocate.

"Do you not remember you are promised to me?" I inquired, lowering my voice for added effect.

If the look she gave me before was horrified, the one she shot my way now was downright ghastly. "You're a liar!" she exclaimed with a gasp, the denial laced with disbelief and a touch of desperation.

I smiled, something I rarely did. "Your father gave me your hand. We wed tomorrow. Tonight, I will show you how to please me. Seraphina!" I snapped my fingers.

The woman in question bounced over and got onto my vast bed. She dutifully unclipped her bra, and her large breasts were unbound. I was about to feast upon them, but as I stood near the edge, she began undoing my pants. She hurriedly freed me and pounced on my dick with her willing, warm mouth. She slid back and forth on it, licking it while it was inside. I threw my head back and began counting. Seraphina was always so eager. Maybe a little too much. I parted my eyes open and gazed at Violet. She looked at me, but something told me she was trying to disregard the sex.

I wagged my finger at her. "Pay attention. I expect you to know how to do this just as well."

Seraphina expertly jacked me and sucked the tip. I could feel the building in my balls. But my eyes were on her hardened nipples, and I licked my lips. "Lay down."

The woman lay obediently on her back, grasping both breasts for me. I seized them from her and sucked on her left areola, then her right. I ran my tongue around the darker pink. I put my face between them and licked the sides and tops.

"Ooo, sire!" she gushed.

I smirked, and I put my fingers in her mouth, which she slurped loudly. She ran her hands over my back and butt, enraptured in passion. She began whimpering like a dog. I had the urge to choke her. I licked her neck, inhaling the sickeningly sweet of her perfume. I sank my fangs into her throat, draining the juicy, delicious blood from her throbbing vein.

"Oh God! I think I'm going to come!" Seraphina screamed.

"Not yet, woman!" I yelled in frustration. I pulled my fingers from her mouth and stuck them in between her legs, quickly finding her clitoris. She was already so wet. She squirmed as I controlled her orgasm. She grabbed my arm, and I increased my stroke of her center.

"I don't need to do this. But since I always aim to have you, I will be nice occasionally. Seraphina loves when I rub her like this."

I resumed sucking the blood from her neck. I squeezed the thin, vein-like structure of her sex between my fingers.

"Yes! Yes! Yes!" Seraphina cried. Her body shuddered violently as I continued stroking her. I pulled my head away, a few droplets of blood falling on my blanket. I let my eyes fall to Seraphina's dilated pupils. "Can we fuck now?" she asked.

I motioned to my captive. "Should we include her?"

Seraphina frowned and pouted. "No, I don't like sharing."

I laughed at her expression; it turned me on. I stood and removed my pants, then pulled off my robe and shirt.

"Lay down, milord," Seraphina said. She stood and slid off her panties.

"Wait." I lay on my back and grabbed my dick. I

unabashedly appraised Seraphina's thick body. She preened and grabbed her large breasts. Then her hands slid across her stomach, over her wide hips, and she bit her bottom lip.

She winked, straddled me, and slid me into her impossibly slick opening. She bounced enthusiastically, her lovely breasts jumping with her. She bit her lip and closed her eyes. I put my hands on her tits and squeezed them. I let her bounce several times before I remembered this was supposed to be a punishment.

"Are you paying attention, Violet? Or shall I call my guards?" I yelled, paying more attention to the little minx fucking me.

"Y-y-yes!" Violet said.

"Squeeze me!" I ordered Seraphina.

"Yes, milord!" she responded breathlessly. She looked up. "You have to squeeze him from the inside. I'll teach you. It feels fucking fantastic!"

"You're gross!" Violet said.

"Wait till you have his dick inside you, you'll change your mind."

I panted. I'd had enough of the uptight bitch. I flipped us and pulled out of Seraphina's wet mound. I got her on her hands and knees; then I entered her. I caught Violet's eye and fucked Seraphina. The pounding of my hips into Seraphina's ass, all while Violet watched, gave me tremendous build-up. My hips became a blur until the only sound was our fucking.

"Yes! God! Harder!" Seraphina cried.

I smacked her ass, loving the sight of the angry red handprint. The buildup was growing. Seraphina's cries were coming more frequent. She was coming too. I pulled her up, still pumping my hips, and sank my fangs into her soft neck again. I sucked with ferocity.

"Jesus!" she screamed as she came. Her tightening caused

me to pull from her abruptly and emit a scream of my own as I came over Seraphina's pale ass.

I breathed hard and glared because Violet was looking away. I would make that bitch pay. I would imprison that fucker Cole and fuck her in front of him.

Cole

The abrupt shaking jolted me awake. I blinked my eyes, attempting to bring the world into focus. The first thing that materialized before me was the countenance of a vampire—pale-faced with piercing green eyes. Slowly, my brows furrowed as I propelled myself upright.

Regrettably, a bad idea.

Immediate dizziness assaulted me. My head spun, and the urge to vomit clawed at my senses. The back of my head throbbed with a pain more intense than before.

"Are you alright, sir?" the man inquired, reaching out to shake me again. Unfortunately, my attempts to lift my head proved futile, leaving me vulnerable and exposed.

"Don't touch me!" I snapped.

"Sir, you are not well. Please allow me to help," he urged, ignoring my plea and grabbing my arm to sit me up.

Anger surged, but my strength deserted me like a fleeing shadow. Then, in a rush, memories flooded back—Violet, our impassioned union, and the sudden ambush. Panic gripped me. Where was she? Despite my resentment, I begrudgingly allowed the vampire to help me sit up, the urgency in his actions mirroring the turmoil within my thoughts.

I scrutinized the vampire before me. His attire was different, not unkempt but distinct—clad in black slacks and a matching shirt. Around his neck hung a gold necklace adorned with a locket. Despite his youthful appearance, the actual age of vampires remained an enigma.

"Did you see them? Do you know what is going on?" I inquired, a bitter taste lingering in my mouth. I spat onto the dry earth.

"Aye! I followed them. They were the generals from the Vampire King's army. They ambushed you and your lady. I pulled you off the road, and they returned to finish you," he explained, his words unveiling a treacherous plot that had unfolded in the shadows.

"What?"

He nodded. "They've been here several times."

"Why should I trust you?"

"The Goddess told me to tell you she sent me for your quest," the vampire said. He pushed his long blonde hair out of his eyes. "My name is Cassius. You can call me Cass."

I eyed the outstretched hand suspiciously.

Blurred memories of Rhys and the snippets of information Rafe said Violet had shared with him churned in my mind. Observing the vampire again, I demanded, "What do you know?"

"We should get you back together with your clan. I couldn't alert them, as they'd kill me on sight," he replied, with urgency in his voice.

"That they would. Help me to my feet," I said. We struggled as I was considerably larger framed than the vampire. I put my arm around Cassius's thin shoulders, expecting to feel his bony structure, but he was stronger than I expected. We edged forward along the path, taking our time. The burning in my heart propelled me on; I had to rescue my love. There was no telling what that freak wanted with her.

And what of this new stranger? The fact that he dragged me off the path worried me. The fact that he knew so much and I would introduce even more strangers to the pack would not go over well, but I needed help.

"Stop right there!" came a deep male voice that I recognized as Daemon. I lifted my head and tried to focus my eyes.

Cassius raised his hands. "I'm just bringing your leader back to you."

Daemon looked confused as he looked from him to me. "Remus, go get reinforcements. Cole's back!"

Observing the shorter werewolf as he made his way deeper into the compound, my head swayed drunkenly at this point. It was a miracle that I hadn't passed out. I leaned heavily on the vampire, who had yet to emit a single grunt; I relied on his support to navigate the unsteady ground beneath me. The compound blurred and warped with each step as the sickness threatened to overwhelm me.

Daemon towered over the vampire, who held his ground without flinching. "What's going on, Cole? Another stranger?" Daemon demanded.

"I was ambushed last night. The vampires took Violet, and I'm in a bad way. What's happened?" I explained.

"Rafe sent out two parties and was gearing up for a third. Sit down. We'll wait," Daemon said, his tone gentler.

With a heavy sigh, I collapsed, breathing heavily. The passage of time became a blur as I remained seated, unable to lift my head. After what felt like an eternity, several werewolves approached. My strength waned, and someone embraced me. My head swam once more in a disorienting liquid haze.

"Thought I'd lost you, brother," Rafe whispered.

"Not yet, I need help."

"We've got the stretcher." A pause. "What of this one?"

I figured he meant the vampire. "He saved my life. I need to speak with him, but I'm dizzy as hell."

"Wolfsbane," Cassius said.

"What?" Rafe asked.

"Yes."

Soon came the disorienting sensation of movement, my eyes involuntarily rolling within their sockets. Suspended on something stretchy, the men carrying me grunted and strained, navigating the arduous task of walking with my inert form. Closing my eyes, I hoped to stave off the queasiness that jostled my stomach.

Soon, we entered my hut. The men halted, preparing to place me on the bed along with the stretcher, but I resisted. Protests erupted around me, yet I sat up. The world swayed beneath me as I stood, and I nearly toppled. A sudden wave of nausea surged, and someone thrust a basket in front of me just in time. A torrent of foul liquid erupted from my mouth, akin to a dragon exhaling fire.

When the unsettling ordeal concluded, I wiped my mouth with the back of my hand and settled onto my bed. Panting, I was aware of a peculiar silence. Raising my gaze, I discovered Rafe, my mother, Ellis, Magnus, and Cassius staring at me with concern and curiosity.

My eyes focused on Cassius. "You gave me something?"

He nodded. "You would've died. I know one thing they gave you was Wolfsbane to diminish your strength. But there was more."

Ellis stepped forward and examined me. It took a minute, but he looked at the vampire too. "You're good. You use moonflower?"

"Yes. I'm a healer where I am from or.... used to be from. I used more enchantments of my design. I've learned a lot."

"Where'd you study?" Ellis asked.

"The Sanctuary of the White Rose."

"With the monks!" Ellis asked, sounding impressed.

"Monks?" I said.

"We'll leave you alone," my mother said. She tapped the still-stunned Ellis and Magnus. Magnus turned, but I halted him.

"Where is Agnus?"

Magnus let out a deep sigh. "We cannot find him. One minute he was here, the next, he'd disappeared. Just like your father did all those years ago before we found him dead."

A chilling wave passed through me, forcing me to steady myself. I met my mother's gaze, finding only sadness in her eyes. The weight of confusion and concern pressed heavily on me—just what the hell was going on? The unsettling parallel between my father's mysterious disappearance and the current situation left an ominous air hanging in the room.

CHAPTER 9

The Gathering Storm

Cole

The vampire and Rafe brought two chairs forward, positioning them closer to me as they transitioned from standing to sitting.

Rafe clarified that the discussion would be put on hold unless I calmed and remained seated. Ellis returned with a solution for me to drink, quickly warming my belly. This elixir also worked wonders on clearing my foggy mind.

"What do we know?" I asked.

"After the festival, we all had breakfast when we noticed you and Violet's absence. We figured you needed... um... some more time, so we gave you that. But we were told by your.... mother you weren't making.... noise, so we checked. When we saw you weren't there and couldn't find you anywhere, we headed out. Twice. I checked your favorite spot. We were preparing to go to the Vampire Kingdom when you and your friend appeared. It was a long shot, but..." Rafe continued but tapered off.

I held up my hand. "I understand. That bastard has Violet, and I'm going to get her back. My question is, what did Rhys give him?"

"He refused to speak to me. He called me a traitor. Listen, old friend, he only means trouble for you. I am afraid we are near the end of peace for our people."

I nodded. "The Goddess visited me in my dreams, has been since I was a boy, but when Violet appeared, I knew what She wanted before She spoke it. The people will never trust me."

"Don't be so sure. They know I remain loyal to you. They didn't stop asking what I was doing to find you..." Rafe smirked. "... And Violet."

My heart jolted. *They've accepted Violet as well? They've forgiven me? How can I repay them?*

"I have the same issue. Had... I should say," Cassius said under his breath.

I looked up at Cassius, tilting my head at him. "Where are you from?"

"I am from the Ashen Coven. We are on the East side of Evernite, not here in the Northern district. The Crimson Keep, that which King Lysander runs, is unruly."

"Why did you move here?" Rafe asked.

"I am a leaf in the wind. I go where I am needed the most. A healer by trade but not given to the biases of my brethren. I was born a vampire, but I am not into most of the things they hold dear: sex, decadence, and all-around sin. I revere solitude and worship the Moon Goddess. She called upon me to approach you and aid you in your quest with Violet," he said.

I frowned. "How did you know you'd succeed?"

"I didn't, but the Goddess can be persuasive. She gives, and she can take." He clutched his locket.

"Aye! I know that well." I touched the back of my head. Then my eyes swiveled to the vampire again. "Do you know what Rhys talked of with the vampire?"

He nodded. "Aye! He's given up the locations of all the werewolf clans in Evernite. Lysander wants to eradicate or enslave them. Starting with yours."

Both Rafe and I stood, eyes wide. "What?" we echoed in unison.

"With that information, all hell will break out. They'll blame us. War between not just us against the vampires but also other clans will happen," Rafe said.

"Men, women, and children will die because of it!" I added.

Rafe looked at me. "Do you think he knows?"

Unlike my earlier sensation, a dreaded emotion enveloped me, and I sank back to the bed. My legs shook slightly.

Long ago, we werewolf pups learned of an ancient artifact called a Talisman of Unity. I didn't know if it was real or imagined, but I thought about it off and on as an adult.

If it is real and the vampires could get a hold of it....

I eyed Rafe. "Let's talk to Rhys."

He nodded and led the way. As we walked through the village, the bustling townspeople paused their daily routines to turn and watch us pass. Some of them murmured their 'hellos,' joy in their eyes. We weaved through the common grounds until we ended in the back of the compound, where we kept the scant prisoners. That hut was larger and rectangle shaped. We entered it, and two guard werewolves stood near the stall where Rhys sat in the cell. He looked up and glared at me.

"Heard you were caught diddling your pet, and they jumped you. Thought they'd rid the kingdom of you for good this time."

I frowned, the weight of the situation pressing upon me.

Clearing my throat, I signaled to the guards, urging them to exit the room.

Cracking my neck, my expression a mix of confusion and hurt. "Do you hate me that much to kill innocent women and children?" The question hung in the air, as it was more than just our camp he threatened.

Rhys eyed me with a look of feigned incomprehension, and a smirk twisted his lips. "I never liked you, Cole. The perfect spawn that could do no wrong. Cole, who never had to work for anything a day in his life. It figures you wouldn't guess shit!"

Disgust crept over me as I shook my head. "What did you give them, Rhys?" I demanded.

He scoffed again, turning his head away in defiance. Growing increasingly impatient, Rafe shouted, "Your Alpha is talking to you! Speak, or I cut off your tongue!"

"And you, Cole's lap dog... have you no spine? Do you like bending to his will?" Rhys sneered.

"Fucker!" Rafe spat, launching himself towards the cell. Instinctively, I had to restrain Rafe, using my strength to prevent him from reaching Rhys.

Rhys rose to his feet, glaring at us insolently. His gaze shifted to the silent vampire observing the scene. "Who's this, Cole? Another pet to take to bed? Tired of the old one so easily?" Rhys taunted.

Having reached my limit, I called out, "Guards!" The urgency in my voice echoed through the room.

The two guards hustled in and stood at attention. "Take this bastard out and brand him. Then take him to the edge of the compound and make sure he leaves," I ordered.

The guards responded promptly. They unlocked the gate and seized Rhys, pulling him out of the structure and leading him outside.

A commotion ensued as a crowd had assembled. Women

clutched their children, the elderly shouted various opinions, and the younger generation was split; some sided with Rhys, others with me.

"Hold on now!" I yelled, trying to quell the rising tumult. The crowd calmed, but the murmurs persisted.

"What is going on, Cole? What has Rhys done?" a woman asked.

"He's betrayed the covenant. I'm banishing him," I declared, the weight of the moment hanging in the air as the crowd absorbed the shocking revelation.

A collective gasp rippled through the onlookers. "What has he done?" an elder inquired, voicing the concerns of the bewildered crowd.

"He gave away secrets to the vampires," Magnus spoke up, his voice carrying a weight beyond his years. He met my gaze with a profound sadness as I looked at him.

"Where is Agnus, Rhys? What have you done to him?" another woman demanded answers.

"I've done nothing wrong. They lie! They don't want anyone to challenge our great Alpha Cole!" Rhys retorted, his laughter carrying a manic edge, echoing through the charged atmosphere like a discordant melody.

As the fire blazed, one guard meticulously stoked it to get the coals just right. He picked up the metal branding iron, displaying the insignia signifying that Cole was to be exiled from the clan. A pang of sorrow reverberated through me, acknowledging that Rhys's heart had turned cold under my leadership. Yet, hadn't it been this way since childhood? I questioned what more I could have done to prevent it, realizing that resigning to him might have been the only course.

Another guard arrived to restrain the struggling Rhys. The other guard, holding the branding iron, approached. My breath caught in my throat as he moved the searing metal toward Rhys. The tension was palpable as the branding iron drew closer.

"Cole!" someone suddenly yelled, the urgent cry cutting through the charged atmosphere.

All eyes had been fixed on the unfolding drama, and a collective gaze shifted upward as a teenager approached. Fear was etched across his face, unadulterated and raw. He gasped for breath as he raced to me, stopping abruptly at my feet. Collapsing, he spoke in a rushed manner, "Agnus... I found Agnus. But something is wrong with him."

A fresh wave of fear gripped my heart, and I grabbed the boy by the shoulders. "Take me to him."

As one, the villagers and I marched towards my hut. My mother emerged from hers, wearing the same look of fear and bewilderment as the boy. I instructed the others to wait and followed her inside. Rafe and Cassius trailed behind me, and the air hummed with anticipation and dread.

When we entered, Agnus sat at the window, his back to it, ostensibly staring at us, yet not quite. His gaze was vacant and distant, the surrounding air carrying a horrendous odor, while a malevolent energy crackled. It bore the unmistakable mark of black magic. Someone or something had laid hold of Agnus, returning him, but an instinct in my mind whispered that this wasn't the same cranky older man.

Cassius stepped around us and examined Agnus, who remained motionless.

"That is not Agnus. What I mean is... it is, but it isn't. He's... wrong," my mother whispered as though she were sharing a secret, her voice tinged with concern and unease.

"What do you think happened to him?" I asked her.

"He smells like your father did, but he had died. There'd been a struggle like your father had fought whatever did this to him. Ellis will not treat him," my mother continued. Her skin had paled. I hugged her.

"There is nothing to treat; he is no more," Cassius concluded.

I frowned and pulled away from my mother to look at him.

"What do you mean? He is living. He is breathing," Rafe said.

"Yes. But this is not a human; it's evil. It's wearing your friend's skin," he said. The look on his face said he was not jesting.

"Oh my God!" my mother exclaimed, and Rafe helped her sit as far away from "Agnus" as possible.

"What do we do?" I asked Cassius.

The vampire frowned, a crease looking out of place on his beautiful face. Then, a realization dawned, and he made the 'ah-ha' face. Without hesitation, he reached into his pants and pulled out a pouch, sprinkling what looked like black sand around the chair where the entity sat, forming a complete, neat circle. Standing, he mumbled incantations, and a puff of smoke emitted from the circle, causing the entity's head to drop forward.

"What did you do?" I asked, my fascination evident.

"I neutralized it. Do you want me to kill it?" he offered, his tone matter-of-fact and ready to act on whatever decision I made.

"Are you going to drain it of blood?" I asked.

"It has no blood. It's evil. If I fed from it, it would overtake me and strip me of my essence, too," Cassius explained.

I frowned. "You have a soul?"

Cassius smirked. "You didn't believe those old wives' tales about vampires having no souls, did you?"

I chuckled nervously. "Actually, I did."

Cassius didn't respond. Instead, he pulled a pouch out of his pants and checked the contents. "I don't have enough. I must return to my abode to retrieve some herbs unless I can collect some from your resident healer?" His tone held a hint of urgency, recognizing the need for a swift resolution to the malevolent presence in our midst.

"Ellis will give you what you need. Tell him I told him to do so."

The vampire nodded and left, but before he turned back. "Whatever you do, don't disturb the circle or go 'near him. I do not know the strength of the evil in that one. But just offhand, I haven't experienced anything like it for some time."

"How long?" I said.

"Long before you were born."

I closed my eyes as Cassius disappeared out the door, the voices of curious villagers reaching my ears on the other side. Protecting them and eliminating this malevolent presence took precedence before I could embark on the mission to rescue Violet. I stood by the door, waiting for Cassius's return.

The passage of two minutes felt like an eternity in the heavy silence. I kept a vigilant eye on my inconsolable mother; tears streamed down her face while Rafe offered comfort. My own emotions tugged at me, but I had to remain focused in case the malignant entity in the room stirred.

When Ellis and Cassius finally entered, I started, the weight of everything that had transpired lifting. They carried bottles and pouches, carefully laying their load on the table alongside a wooden bowl and spoon. Without a word, they began mixing a concoction, working quickly and quietly as the room held its collective breath.

"How long has it been?" Ellis asked, stealing a nervous glance over his shoulder.

"Five or six minutes. We have time," Cassius replied.

Without warning, the entity snorted, raised its head, and opened its eyes—now pitch black. The chair began to shake violently. My mother shrieked, leaping off the floor to stand on her bed, and Rafe backed away, shielding her.

"What's going on?" I yelled as the wind outside began to howl.

Cassius eyed me solemnly. "It's waking." He picked up the bowl and approached the jolting demon. Thunder rumbled, and lightning flashed outside. The villagers' screams reached our ears. I opened the door to pandemonium—women and children scattered, screaming.

"Get to your huts and stay there till I say!" I shouted, but my words were likely lost amidst the chaos. I slammed the door shut, the tumult outside now muffled, leaving us in the tense silence of the room where the malevolent force continued to stir.

Cassius stood resolutely over the demon, dipping his finger into the mixture and painting an oily cross on the demon's forehead. The creature growled, fighting against its mystical bindings, displaying a strength far beyond that of an old, feeble man. The skin on its face began to peel where the cross had been placed, revealing a grotesque transformation.

The vampire chanted loudly over the demon's shrieks and struggles. "Vanquish me, eh?" came the driest, raspiest voice I'd ever heard––the demon was speaking.

"You are not wanted here. Go back to the Hell you came from!" Cassius shouted.

The demon laughed, a hacking, even drier sound. "Your charms and spells cannot stop me. I've awakened, and awake I shall stay. I will wrench your soul from your bones, bloodsucker!" In an instant, its hand wrapped around the vampire's throat, and the demon opened its mouth wide.

Wider.

The demon's mouth stretched wider than I had ever seen as if preparing to detach its jaw and swallow the vampire whole. Panic surged within me—I couldn't let harm come to the vampire. Determined, I ran up to the struggling pair. As I reached out to grip the demon's hand, it instantly recoiled, emitting a horrendous howl.

"Cole Wilderwolf!"

My mother gasped, and Rafe stared in shock. The vampire, amid the chaos, eyed me, appearing oddly at ease, as if he had experienced this many, many times before. The demon continued its shrieks, directing its malevolence squarely at me.

"He bested me once. He will never again!" the demon roared. The next second, everything ceased—no more noise. The demon's head fell back, and it stopped moving. I panted, realizing I had been holding my breath. Something told me he was talking about my father. This thing faced off with my dad and was bested. Would it seek revenge?

"Oh my God! That thing knew Romulus?" my mother asked. She was always so observant.

I didn't answer her as I looked at Rafe. He helped my mom sit as she was standing against the wall. Her eyes were puffy. She sniffled and buried her head in Rafe's neck. He stiffly comforted her, but how could he?

"Well, I think I know what that thing was, but I have to go to my home and get my things. Should I come back?" Cassius asked.

"Yes. Bring your things here. We will accompany you," I said.

He nodded and left.

I ran a hand through my hair, contemplating the empty vessel that had once housed a living, breathing werewolf. Despite our strained relationship, no one deserved to have their soul sucked from their body. As I pondered what to do with the lifeless form, it slowly began to deflate like a balloon, emitting a sickly hissing sound. The body slid to the floor, and then, with an eerie disappearance, it was gone.

There was a knock on the door. "Come in!" I bellowed.

Daemon came in. He bowed to me. "You should come out, sir."

"What in the name of Mother Moon now," I grumbled.

"It's not good, sir," he said.

With a sinking feeling, I followed him out, Rafe hot on my heels. My mother followed, too. The sky had cleared, and night was quickly approaching. The men had gathered, arguing with each other. Five men stood near the two guards, still holding a now-bound Rhys. The other men faced them, all of them shouting and taunting one another. When we came out, everyone quieted.

"What's going on?" I asked.

"It's a mutiny, Your Lordship," Rhys said with a smirk.

"What?" I asked, not believing him.

"I said I want to duel. Rakzyrno!" he declared.

My eyes widened, and my heart shattered into millions of pieces. A collective gasp echoed through the crowd, including my mother, who cried out in despair. When he uttered those words, he cursed one of us to die. Fighting in Rakzyrno meant fighting to the death, with the victor becoming the next Alpha.

My frown deepened as I glared at the cocky grin of the bastard, Rhys. He'd brought a plague on this community greater than anything Violet could've dreamed. His lies and accusations had divided us, and it was now my responsibility to bridge the gap, to renew the hope that had sorely snaked its way through our clan. This infection threatened to spread to other factions, but I vowed to stop it here. I was the cure.

CHAPTER 10

Torn Between Worlds

Violet

The rhythmic drip of water echoed through the room, both a source of comfort and annoyance. Bound and confined in what appeared more like a chamber than a dungeon, my senses were on high alert. I strained my ears for the distinctive sound of footsteps, his footsteps—the ones belonging to King Lysander. After the unsettling spectacle of his intimate encounter with his mistress and the subsequent threats, his guards were summoned, and I found myself thrust into this peculiar space. It's not a dungeon but a sex dungeon.

It struck me as odd. Despite the degradation and confinement, a strange detachment settled over me. My mind flickered with fragmented memories, elusive and slippery. They teased me with glimpses of actions I couldn't fully grasp. Every attempt to hold on to those fleeting thoughts proved futile as they dissipated like mist, leaving me grappling with a frustrating amnesia.

The moment they bound me, and yes, they had tightly secured my restraints in this room, my head drooped again, and my body relaxed while I drifted off yet again.

I dash through a sunlit glade, the sky above painted in a dazzling blue canvas devoid of fluffy white clouds. A gentle breeze carries the fragrant wildflowers and the aftermath from a recent rainstorm. My bare feet connect with the earth, each step pushing me forward in a desperate escape. The beat of my heart quickens, resonating with a sense of urgency.

The surroundings exude perpetual perfection, an idyllic landscape stretching beyond my vision. This unblemished beauty has been my reality for as long as my extensive memory allows me to recall. The weight of knowledge in my mind presses down, burdening me with an unspoken truth. Tears blur my vision, yet I press on, propelled by an unseen force.

Run!

The whisper in my head amplifies, a loud and insistent cadence. Are they following? Questions swirl, yet my brain guards the answers like a closely held secret. All I can fathom is the stark reality that chaos will unfurl if I dare to stop, if I let them perceive that I am aware. The weight of the unknown presses on, urging me forward, a silent plea to keep moving through the pristine glade, my sanctuary on the edge of unraveling.

Hurry!

I forge ahead, crossing a frigid river that sends a shock through my system as the icy water envelopes my bare feet. Unyielding, I refuse to pause, even as I slide on the moss-coated surface of a submerged rock. The sting of my scuffed skin jolts through me, tempting me to inspect the injury. Yet, I resist the urge, my gaze fixed upward at the expanse of the sky.

She came to me. Whispers of a secret passed between us, a revelation now burdening my every step. Could it be true? The fate of humanity rests squarely on my shoulders. I sense an impending ritual, a duty that demands completion—a weighty responsibility to halt everything. The dreadful truth I bear must remain veiled, a secret that no one else need carry.

"Violet!" a voice screams, piercing through the haze, and I break into a run.

I shake my head, glancing behind me, but there's nothing there. Whose voice is calling out to me?

"Wake up, Violet!" the same voice insists.

I need to escape. Now!

Suddenly, I am shaken, and my eyes snap open. I find myself face to face with the pale-faced vampire, an infuriating smirk etched on his features. He's dressed in his usual arrogant attire--leather pants paired with a silk black shirt--but the robe is absent. His long blonde hair is meticulously styled, framing his pale face, and his lips bear a crimson hue as if he's wearing makeup. Unyielding, his hard brown eyes lock onto mine, leaving me with a shiver. I turn away, haunted by visions of the man who betrayed me. But deep inside, I sense that not everything is as it seems.

"Lost in a nightmare? Hmm? Don't worry all of that will be over when the ritual is performed. You'll love being a vampire... and a Queen," he said. He was arranging his sexual weapons on the wall.

I remained silent, focusing on the medallion around my neck. A whisper, an intuition, told me I was stronger than it, stronger than him. I would escape.

"Not going to speak?" Lysander taunted.

I sighed, contemplating what could be alluring about this vampire besides his wealth. He appeared feeble, like something waterlogged--a stark contrast to Cole, who exuded strength, courage, and power.

"What's on your mind?" Lysander persisted. He approached me, and though I avoided eye contact, he seized my chin in a painful grip, reminding me of the strike of a cobra. "You will obey."

I gathered a substantial amount of spit in my mouth and spat in his face. The moisture landed, and he wiped his eyes. In retaliation, he backhanded me.

"You disobey me, you wench?" he snarled.

"Isn't that obvious?"

"Then you must be punished." He turned and walked toward the opposite wall, in a presumed effort to find something to use for my punishment. It was now or never. I focused on my power, closing my eyes and calling to it. To my surprise, I quickly connected with it. It filled my being, causing the hair on my limbs to stand on end, and my blood hummed with its essence. My right wrist was chained to the board, but I concentrated on my power, building it deep in my belly. It churned, bubbled, and mixed, ready for release.

Lysander suddenly turned like he could sense my actions. "What are you doing?" Lysander sneered.

I ignored him. Full concentration engulfed me, and the surge of power was intoxicating, leaving my head fuzzy, filled with static. Suddenly, the energy charged, flooding my extremities.

"You idiot, you can't get free. Your power is..." Lysander started to say, but even he fell silent.

With raw control, I pulled my arm from the backing, the chain dangling as if it were made of rubber. I tilted my head.

"You! You cannot do this! You're..." Lysander whispered, shock etched on his already pale face, his hand covering his mouth.

My body began to emit a luminescence of its own, and the chains, the medallion, and the locks fell to the floor. I was freed. Stepping away from the board, I calmly turned to leave the stupefied king. Suddenly, a firm hand clamped on my shoulder, and I turned.

"You uncouth wench, I'll teach you!" he snarled.

Frowning, I harnessed the power of my mind and lifted him off the ground, his desperate cries for guards filling the air. With a forceful motion, I hurled him against the unforgiving wall.

Two guards hurried in, and I turned to face them. They pulled out their swords and charged. I bent the first one's sword with my mind; the other used this as his opportunity to attack. His blade sliced at my shoulder. The nerve ending sang with pain pummeling my brain. Panting, I lifted my hand, levitating the second damnable vampire off his feet and throwing him against the wall, too.

Without hesitation, I hurried from the room before more guards could arrive. As I found the stairs, the footsteps thundered like a stampede headed in my direction. Reversing my direction, I streaked by the room in a blur, fleeing my captors' clutches with hallways twisting maze-like before me. They hadn't made it up the stairs, but I could only go up or into another room. Choosing to go up, I hoped to find another way out.

Cole

The night had cloaked the day, and the entire clan, except for the slumbering children, gathered with bated breath. The crowd formed a solemn circle in a clearing beneath the waning moon. Rhys and I stood on opposite sides, clad only in pants; the cool wind brushed against my bare chest. Anxious eyes stared back at me from the crowd. Most were on my side, aware that this would mark the end of Rhys—everyone sure, except me. Did I possess the fortitude to take his life?

"Come on, mighty leader! I haven't got all night. I need my beauty rest. Tomorrow is a grand day, for I will lead the people better than you!" Rhys taunted.

"All bark and no bite, as expected," I scoffed, glaring at him. "An Alpha leads through wisdom, not empty boasting."

Rhys scoffed. "We'll see who leads after I tear your heart out!"

"You lack the patience and discipline of a true Alpha," I countered. "Throw your life away if you must, but the pack will not follow a mindless brute."

"They'll follow me when they see your blood soaking the ground!"

"You are not worthy of this fight, but I shall grant you the lesson you seem to crave."

He crouched, ready to strike. "Come, meet your fate."

Magnus strode between us, his somber eyes imparting a grave meaning. He lifted his aged, frail hand overhead. As I shut my eyes, the metamorphosis began in a frenzied burst. The rip of fabric, the crack of bones, the sloshing of organs settling into place—it all happened swiftly. My eyes changed, and I howled on all fours, joining the eerie chorus of Rhys' snarls. His fur displayed a mix of dark and light brown, eyes gleaming with a mesmerizing shade of yellow. Slobber dripped from his gaping maw as he roared.

My transformation manifested with light and dark gray fur, accompanied by iced blue eyes. I was double the size of Rhys. We approached each other cautiously, circling in the clearing. Rhys lunged at me, maw snapping and claws raised high. I leaped into the air, swiping my front paw, clubbing him in the face. He collided with the ground, rolling in frustration as he got back up and attempted another attack. I bounded out of the way, evading his assault. Rhys lunged at me once more, his teeth bared, and I dodged to the side. The surrounding forest echoed with our growls and the rustling of leaves. I circled him, eyes fixed on his every move. He charged again, claws extended, but I met him head-on this time. We collided with a force that shook the ground.

Locking jaws, we wrestled in the moonlit glade. His strength was formidable, but my determination matched it. I flipped him onto his back, taking advantage of the moment. Rhys snarled and kicked, attempting to break free. As he writhed beneath me, I couldn't ignore the conflict within. This was the same werewolf who had once been my friend, my brother-in-arms. Now, he was a traitor, and I had to stop him.

We disengaged momentarily, circling each other again. Rhys came at me with renewed aggression. I dodged and countered, each of us exchanging blows. The fight was fierce, a dance of fangs and claws under the moon's watchful gaze. As the battle raged on, the forest held its breath.

Rhys landed a deep gash on my side, and I winced in pain. However, the injury only fueled me. With a burst of strength, I tackled him to the ground. Pinning him, I locked eyes with the wolf who had once been my comrade.

As my heart withered, the urgency to conclude this fight was all-consuming. The madness and murderous intent in Rhys's eyes fueled my resoluteness. My paws faltered for a minute, and Rhys struck, his claw viciously slashing my face. A roar of pain erupted from me as a reflex, and I retaliated, slicing into his exposed chest before swiftly bounding away.

The air became thick with the rich scent of blood, its metallic tang filling my snout. The crowd, a chorus of judgment, whispered their thoughts as Rhys closed in with relentless speed, the noise of his rapid approach drowning out all else. I rolled over as he pounced, his powerful jaws snapping at me. Our struggle intensified, a clash of might against might. I would have cried out in wolf form if I could, but all that escaped was another fierce roar.

Rhys seized the opportunity, freeing one of his paws and driving his claws into my side, inflicting a deep and agonizing wound. Another roar erupted from me, a symphony of pain echoing through the glade. And out of desperation to end the agony, I sliced my nails across Rhys' bared throat, nicking the jugular vein.

My breaths were heavy as the wolf, rapidly transforming back into a man, retreated from me. I, too, began to shift into my human form, each breath a struggle. Bloodied, battered, and writhing in pain, I sat up and stood. Despite the anguish coursing through me, I walked over to Rhys and stood over his weakened form. He lay there, barely clinging to life, one hand pressed against his fatal wound. In a feeble motion, he gestured toward me.

Kneeling beside him, I leaned in, my ear close to his mouth —a final act of mercy to a dying werewolf.

"I'm sorry," he croaked, each word strained through labored breaths.

I nodded, a heavy acknowledgment. "Did you give away the locations for real?" I needed to know.

He slowly shook his head. "I hate them more than I hate you..." He chuckled at the ill-timed humor.

I shook my head as tears welled up. "I love you too," I whispered so only he could hear.

Rhys' eyes filled with tears, and he struggled with the words. ".... goodbye... friend..." Rhys drew his final breath, his eyes staring unseeing. I closed his lids and lowered my head in solemn respect.

A collective hush fell over us as everyone converged on the aftermath of the brutal fight. My mother rushed over, her touch gentle on my face. Tears streamed as I gazed into her eyes. In an embrace, I let out the emotions that had been building, weeping into the crook of her neck. Her arms tightened around me, but I winced in pain.

"Oh, my Goddess, I forgot about your wound!" she exclaimed.

Men approached with a stretcher, and I attempted to protest, but Rafe intervened, insisting on my care. Reluctantly, I got on the stretcher, as they also loaded Rhys's body onto another one. I exchanged a look with Rafe, understanding that Rhys would be laid to rest among our departed.

They hurried me into my hut, where immediate attention was given to my injuries. I had a splitting headache and weakness in my body from the toll of the fight. Ellis and Cassius appeared, the latter taking over from my mother, who had to be led away as her grief overwhelmed her. Cassius handed me a mixture to drink and attended to my wounds with skilled hands. Ellis observed with evident admiration for the vampire's speed and expertise.

I made a face after drinking the chalky mixture, but my vitality returned. My muscles relaxed like I had taken a long hot bath, something we werewolves weren't accustomed to. Cassius wanted to monitor my wounds, so we talked about the fight, and I filled him in on the gravity of everything that had to deal with the duel. He was impressed, saying many cultures had something like that.

Two foggy hours passed in a blur, and I finally felt as I did before the ruthless brawl. Ellis and Cassius examined me thoroughly before approving me to prepare for the mission to rescue Violet. I sent Rafe to gather the men while I bid farewell to my mother.

"You understand why I have to do this, Mom?" I asked.

Her tear-filled eyes met mine. "Oh, Cole, I almost lost you just now. Must I worry all night for you?" she whispered.

I kissed her forehead. "I am a warrior, Mom. Shall I leave her with the King?"

She sniffled. "No. Take care, baby." She kissed my cheek. "He would be so proud."

I kissed her cheek, too, and headed out. As I walked, the weight of the upcoming challenges settled on my shoulders. Would he truly be proud to know I'd slain my best friend and was about to rescue a witch? I pushed the doubts aside.

When I emerged into the clearing leading to the center, most of our hundreds of men had assembled. Some carried weapons, all dressed in war attire with helmets and shields. They fell silent as I strode towards them, and when I stepped onto the stage, they remained standing, awaiting my command.

"Hail Bloodmoon Brothers!" I greeted them.

"Hail!" they said in unison.

"Thank you for coming. I do not know where I went wrong with Rhys, but I never intended to divide us. I hope to keep us united and serve as humbly as possible. I have done my best to provide for my family and loved ones. Tonight, what happened will not happen again. I will not tolerate dissent in my pack. It is important now more than ever before that we fight as one. A united pack. As you all should know, the vampires kidnapped my mate Violet last night. I intend to get her back by any means necessary. I do not demand to make anyone do anything against their wishes. If you do not want to go, lay down your weapons and walk away. I will not blame you." I waited a minute. No one moved apart from looking at each other. "Fine. Tonight, we move on to Lysander's lands. He may expect us, but he's an idiot, so we may still have the upper hand. We converge like the graceful ants, mobilized, and controlled. My gut tells me they are probably throwing a stupid party, and with all those snobs milling about, we can easily breach the open gates of the castle. I know that is where

Violet is. Get her and get out of the building. Only use force when needed. Never underestimate those bastards and err on the side of caution. Does everyone understand?"

The men nodded in unison, their declarations echoing as they raised their swords. Stepping off the stage, I nearly collided with Cassius, who now sported a different outfit and carried a sword and shield.

Frowning, I asked, "You're fighting your kind?"

"My kind died a long time ago. Let's go get your mate, friend," Cassius replied.

"How can we trust this one, Cole?" a man asked from the crowd. Several men shouted their agreement.

I held up my hand. "I know this is not our way. But Cass has proved trustworthy until now. Though if he shows otherwise on the battlefield, you have my permission to kill him, fair?"

The men murmured amongst themselves.

"That sounds fair to me," the vampire shouted. "Come on, let's get going!"

His declaration did something I wasn't expecting. Several men started banging their lance handles against the ground.

I smiled at the vampire, and he grinned back. Then, we all stealthily snuck off into the night, ready for the impending rescue mission.

CHAPTER 11

The Power Within

Violet

Concealed in the corner's shadows behind the door, I had lingered for ten tedious minutes as the dim-witted guards scoured in vain while their fool king barked commands. My palms itched to demolish the contemptible castle as the oafs thundered about. I began to stir from my hiding spot when a figure crossed the threshold. Correction—two silhouettes entered the chamber.

"The wench dares make a fool of me? Shocking that Jacob had the nerve to lie outright before a king," Lysander fumed.

"You were aware, sire?" a woman questioned.

"Naturally. I have my reasons for sparing him. As you know, I require a sorceress of unrivaled power for this unification. She will be my instrument, the daft slut. She's erased it all!" he raged.

"Self-inflicted, I suspect. She spells your doom, my lord. I implore you, reconsider. Never have I witnessed such might as she wields. And she is no mere spell caster. The prophecy foretells..."

"Sire! Werewolves approaching the perimeter!" a man informed everyone.

Werewolves? Oh, Goddess! Cole! I must find him.

"Muster the guards! Engage them, fool!" Lysander bellowed.

Retreating steps echoed away.

"We shall resume this later," he snapped. Stiff rustling fabrics sounded, and more footsteps faded—one pair.

"You may emerge," the female voice said in a bored voice.

My pulse quickened twofold. I swallowed, stepped out from behind the door, and faced a new vampiress. Magic and vigor radiated from her being. With dark chestnut tresses and warm amber eyes, her beauty was perpetually preserved in her transformed state.

"I am Isabella, the seer here. And you must be Violet. Yes, I can see it in your eyes." Her gaze swept over me. "Quite beautiful. I sense formidable power within you. Why block your memory so?"

I frowned in confusion. "What?"

"You blocked your memory."

"No, I-I don't..." That fleeing dream returned of me sprinting away. From what? Or whom?

"Something dreadful compelled you to forget, I expect. That window has a tree outside. You must climb down and find him soon. Lysander fights dirty," she warned.

I frowned. "Why help me?"

"For the moment. Lysander grasps not what he risks. A primordial evil has awakened, far worse than vampires or werewolves. You are needed. I wish to survive," she stated.

I stared, gripped by a sudden terror. Some buried intuition told me her words rang true.

"Hey!" She snapped her fingers before my face. I jolted alert. "Go, now!"

I nodded and rushed to the window she'd indicated, pausing as she sauntered out. I shook off my daze; I hiked up my skirt and prepared to scale the tree.

Cole

We fanned out, continuing our stealthy advance as we descended upon Lysander's domain like a wave of shadows. Mother Moon withheld her radiance behind an ominous veil of clouds cloaking our approach. The men moved with disciplined speed and silence like we had done this before. Our ancestors had, long ago, when these lands were also ours––before hordes of vampires swarmed in, turning or slaying my people. I was thankful to be spared witnessing that carnage and intended to avoid it tonight.

Nearing the township, I halted our force. I dispatched twenty troops in each direction and led my group straight for the stronghold. We coursed through vacant streets fast, the late hour granting little resistance. Only a scarce few vampires roamed about, fleeing at our sight. Undeterred, we pressed onward.

We were halfway across the courtyard when a swarm of vampires led by a fierce warrior emerged from the keep. "Going somewhere, mutts?" their leader growled, swords drawn as they advanced.

I unsheathed my blade, signaling my warriors to form up.

"We've come for my mate. Stand aside, and no blood needs to spill tonight," I warned.

The vampire horde responded with snarls and jeers. "The witch is long gone! And soon, you beasts will join her! And you've taken in the weird one, eh?"

I turned my head to look beside me to see who they were talking about, and beside Rafe was Cassius. He looked calm and collected, as always.

"You dare mock me as odd while you sloppily gorge on human flesh? I have perfected the art of taking only what I need from the beasts of the forest. In a thousand years, I have never fully drained a vessel—their lives are not mine to take." Cassius glared with disdain at the foolish vampire, gripping the hilt of his ancient blade. "Speak again in ignorance, and I shall gladly remove your tongue."

Laughter erupted from the werewolves surrounding me.

The head vampire's brows furrowed, and the vampires surged forward without another word, launching themselves at our group. We collided in a clash of steel, fangs, and claws. I cut through two vampires while also suffering wounds from their razor-like nails. My warriors fought like heroes, but the vampires outnumbered us in close quarters.

I rallied my men to retreat towards the gates. We forged our battle through the courtyard, leaving many vampire bodies in our wake without too many losses. We spilled back into the streets to turn the tide, racing for the tree line.

We regrouped in the woods, and I turned to my warriors. "It seems Violet has been moved, or these freaks are lying. I wouldn't put it past them. But this is only the opening battle———we will gather reinforcements and strategies. Then Lysander will pay." Howling sounded in the distance, signaling the other factions of my force. The real fight was just beginning. I needed to buy time for the others to join us.

"Defensive positions!" I ordered. "They'll be coming!"

No sooner had we hunkered behind stones and trunks than a fresh wave of vampires spilled from the stronghold gate, weapons glinting in the moonlight. Arrows whistled from the trees, felling several of the bloodsuckers before they reached our lines.

The clash of fangs, claws, swords, and shields resounded through the woods as the vampires fell upon us. I crushed one's windpipe with my claws while severing another's head clean off with one mighty sword stroke. My warriors fought with equal savagery, sending limbs and dark blood flying.

The vampires kept coming, their numbers appearing endless. The duel's toll and the sword's swinging tired my weakened limbs, but still, I raged on. The bloodsuckers forced us deeper into the woods; we were losing ground. I rallied my warriors to stand firm, even as deadly claws and blades cut into us.

A hulking vampire juggernaut broke through our ranks, making straight for me. I braced myself, delivered a fatal uppercut, and almost decapitated the brute. Its corpse slumped at my feet, but two more fiends took its place. Between the war, I looked for any sign of my love. She was nowhere to be seen.

As the battle raged on, I fought with all my might, my mind torn between the immediate threat and the desperate search. The moonlit chaos intensified as the clash of weapons and the screams of combatants echoed through the woods.

My warriors, despite their resilience, were growing weary. We couldn't hold out forever against the relentless tide of vampires. The forest became a labyrinth of chaos and bloodshed, with warriors falling into the fray on both sides. I spotted a figure during the conflict, a vampire who carried an air of authority. Could he be the one leading this assault? Determined, I slashed my way toward him, deflecting attacks from his underlings as I went. The vampire leader, however, proved to be a formidable opponent.

Our blades clashed in a series of strikes and parries. The battle pressed on me from all sides, squeezing breath from my lungs and clarity from my mind until only my pack's survival and Violet's rescue mattered. In my distraction, my opponent's blade nicked my shoulder.

I winced and glared at his smug face. "You'll pay for that, bloodsucker!"

"Will I? Learn your place, damnable dog!" he said, slashing at me again.

In an instant, a surge of energy pulsed through the air. Magic. Cassius, our enigmatic vampire ally, emerged from the shadows. "I've come to turn the tide, lad," he declared, eyes locked with mine. With a wave of his hand, he unleashed a burst of mystical energy that repelled the vampires, creating a temporary barrier.

"Find your mate swiftly, Cole Wilderwolf," Cassius urged. "I shall hold them off for now. But time is of the essence."

Grateful for the unexpected distraction, I nodded in acknowledgment and motioned for my men to follow. We stopped behind some boulders to regroup again. Every able-bodied werewolf in beast and man joined the meeting. Some dragged our fallen behind, too. In the clearing, the vampires shouted to one another——regrouping.

"Where could she have gone?" Rafe asked, his chest heaving.

"Could she be headed back? Was this all for naught?" came a soldier's voice.

"I told you we're here for Violet, and I won't stop until I find her," I declared, leaving. But Rafe halted me.

"We'll find her together, brother!" he affirmed.

My keen earshot caught the whistling of an arrow. Moonlight shone as I saw it hurtling toward Rafe. I shoved him aside, and the arrow pierced my side. I cried out in agony.

"Cole!" Rafe screamed, catching me as I collapsed. Fiery pain blazed from the wound. I sagged against Rafe as he pulled me back. He ordered the men out to fight while caring for me. By the Goddess' grace, the pain receded some. But Rafe's expression told me it was grave.

"That bad, huh?" I rasped, wincing even at breathing.

"Don't you die on me, you oaf. I can't haul you back," he whispered, choking up.

Goddess, is this how I die? Violet, love, where are you? I can't go without seeing your lovely face again.

"Take care of yourself...and marry Camille, for God's sake," I murmured.

He sniffled, trails of tears cleaning his grimy face. I lifted a trembling hand to wipe them away. He clasped my fingers. Dawn approached, having failed all--my father, Rhys, Mother, Rafe, Agnus, Magnus... Violet, most of all. I closed my eyes, readying to die.

Violet

I must find him! I have to find him!

I rushed forward, breaths coming in hurried pants. Feet pounding against the ground. The vampires were locked in fierce battle. Momentarily, they diverted their attention. A gut-wrenching cry pierced the night air—Cole's name shouted in anguish.

And in my head, he whispered, *Goodbye, love.*

A gasp caught in my throat. My heart ceased its rhythmic beating. I pivoted swiftly, sprinting toward that agonized call without a second thought. Moonlight carved a luminous path, guiding my way through the darkness. I gathered my skirts, pushing myself faster. Urgency fueled my steps. Fear gripped me that time was slipping. I had to reach him. Each stride brought me closer to the chilling cry. Cole's name still echoed in my mind. I blinked back tears, willing my legs to move quicker.

Oh, Goddess! I can't lose him!

I arrived at the open clearing, gasping for breath. My swift journey had drained me. The werewolves' focus were directed away, granting momentary concealment. I advanced cautiously, tears streaming, stifling a sob. They finally sensed my presence—a tap on the shoulder of the one in front. My bare, battered feet went unnoticed, numb to pain. Only my heart ached.

I will perish if he's dead.

The men parted, revealing a heart-wrenching scene. Rafe cradled Cole's limp form, head hung low in weeping. Despite the battle, all I could hear was Rafe's anguish. Yet some invisible force drew his attention. Reluctantly, he lifted his eyes to meet mine. Sorrow marked his face. Tears and dirt streaked his skin. Overwhelmed by the devastation, I sank to the ground. Rafe sensed my depthless grief. He rose, placing Cole's head in my lap. A primal wail escaped my soul's depths. My core's buried origin. My magic churned and boiled.

"You can't die, my love! Don't leave me," I whispered.

He didn't respond.

Panic hit me, and I shrieked, "Cole! Don't you leave me!" I hit his chest, but he would not rouse.

A sudden vibration surged through me. I clung to Cole's lifeless form in desperation, fearing my magic. Fearing facing life alone. Energy swelled within. Growing powerful, more potent. With a primal scream, I threw back my head. The force so mighty the earth rumbled. The heavens themselves trembled. Blinding light erupted from within. All fighting halted. The moon's gentle glow reflected off me in every direction. Werewolves near me shielded their eyes from the intense radiance. I was captivated by the scene on the illuminated battlefield.

The vampires, caught in Mother Moon's rays of moonlight and the ethereal glow emanating from my body, erupted into tortured screams and began to smoke. The haunting echoes of their agony reverberated through the night, and in the relentless onslaught of light, not a shred of their clothing remained.

I gazed at my beloved, preparing for a last farewell as I lifted him gently, leaning to press a kiss to his beautiful lips. Yet, something was amiss—his lips weren't cold but warm against mine. A profound shock coursed through me when his hand rose to cradle my head, and a groan escaped his lips. Startled, my eyes shifted downward to find the arrow that had once pierced his side had vanished, disintegrated into nothingness.

Cole removed his bloodied shirt with a wry smile, revealing unblemished, smooth skin. Grinning into his bright blue eyes, I was overwhelmed by a surge of joy. We embraced, the radiant light surrounding us gradually fading. We broke apart, Cole's eyes dropped to my lips, a silent invitation. As he moved in to kiss me again, Rafe gasped.

"Cole, you done my heart in! You're alive!" Rafe yelled, snatching him from my lips just before ours met.

Everyone turned and converged on us. They clapped Cole on the back or ruffled his hair, with Rafe giving him a hearty hug last. I embraced them both. The crowd cheered as Cole and I stood together.

"Victory is ours!" Cole declared, holding up our clasped hands in triumph. The crowd chanted in celebration as we all turned to head back to camp. Cole threaded our fingers and led me along.

"You die on me again, and I'll kill you!" I threatened.

He chuckled. "Duly noted, love." He raised our hands and kissed mine.

I tossed my hair over my shoulder, glancing back one last time at the Vampire King's lands, sure I would never return.

CHAPTER 12

The Sum of All Things

Violet

"Listen to me!" he hissed.

"No! I am no longer tied to you. It's over. We won!" I cried.

"No, you insipid girl. You belong with me. You belong to me. Come to me.... Now!" he said, sounding more and more like a snake. I could even hear the rattle of his tail.

"How are you doing this? Let me go! I do not love you. I do not want you!" I sobbed.

"It isn't about love. This is about power! You have more than you know, and I want it! Now come to me before I annihilate everything you hold dear!" he shouted.

"I am no longer afraid. He has power. I have power. Together, we will end you!"

The voice in the dark just laughed. It echoed, sounding like multiple people.

"Laugh now, cry later," I taunted.

"What are you talking about?" There was a hint of unease in his tone now.

"I will remember everything. I will know everything, and I will end you," I said with confidence.

"Does he know of our blood bond?"

Coldness spread throughout my belly, replacing the comfort I'd just felt. "We have no bond."

"You can lie to yourself, and you can lie to him, but you cannot lie to me. We are tethered, and you will come. You will listen. You will obey."

I gasped awake, my heart pounding. The vivid dream lingered like a shadow in my mind. A blood bond...with the Vampire King? Revulsion washed over me at the thought. Could it be true? I shakily touched the healed puncture wounds on my neck. If we were bonded by blood, did that mean he could control me? Summon me? Fear gripped my insides at the implications.

What else had he done to me while I was under his power? Missing memories taunted me, just out of reach. Doubt crept in, poisoning my joy. I wanted to tell Cole, to be safe in his arms. But confessing this would only frighten him. No, I could not place this burden on my love. Not yet. Not until I understood what had happened... and how to undo it. I shivered, alone with my dark discoveries.

The dream had shattered my hard-won sense of freedom. But I could not let dread overwhelm me. When the time came, I would find the strength to break any claim the Vampire King held over me. Somehow, I had to believe that, even as foreboding threatened to smother all hope. I closed my eyes, trying to remember something, but all I could think of was the crude act between him and his mistress. I began tingling between my thighs.

When we'd returned, some men wanted to keep celebrating deep into the night. But Cole wavered on his feet, so he and I opted to retire to bed. We fell asleep almost immediately after sharing a brief kiss. But now my body craved his.

I sat up and looked at Cole's sleeping form in the pale morning light. His chest was bare, his hand tucked under his head. Clad only in dark brown pants, he looked beautiful in his vulnerability. I smirked, gazing at him like that first glimpse so long ago. I reached out, cleared the hair off his strong forehead, and traced my finger along the Roman nose that perfectly suited his face. My finger continued over his pronounced Cupid's bow, resting on his thick, beautiful lips.

I sighed, about to turn away, but as my hand moved, he reached out and grabbed it. He planted a kiss on the palm, all with his eyes closed. My mouth hung open in shock.

"Morning," he said, his voice thickened with sleep. He cleared his throat. Still, the man didn't open his eyes.

"How can I tell what you are thinking if you won't open your eyes?" I asked, a smile creeping on my face.

"You can never tell what a man is thinking, love. Only that he is alive or dead," he remarked.

I laughed. "You have had the pleasure of being both. What was death like?"

His eyelids raised. There was a seriousness in his eyes. "Quiet but comforting. Like being wrapped in a blanket."

I tilted my head at him, wondering if he wanted to talk about it. But he said nothing, staring off.

Was it time to tell him about my bond with the Vampire King? I was torn.

"What's wrong?" he asked.

I smiled. "You're a lot like your mother."

He grinned, and his entire face lit up like Lindy's, too. He was so overwhelmingly handsome. Between my thighs began to throb. I bit my bottom lip.

He raised a thick brow. "Do you want me?"

I nodded. He motioned for me to come closer, and we met in a passionate kiss. The next thing I knew, his thick tongue was in my mouth, and my hands were in his long, black hair, drawing him closer. We rolled where I was under his immense body. I wrapped my legs around his waist, the nub at my center stimulated by something on his pants. I moaned as our tongues wrestled. He ran his hands through my hair, along my back, till his hands were on my butt. I began grinding my center on the protrusion from him. His hands ran along my thighs, my senses heightened, and my brain plunged deep in liquified rhapsody.

Suddenly, he rolled us over so I was on top of him, and I was so tiny, barely covering his gigantic frame. I sat up, smiling at him. He placed his large hands on my waist.

I reached up and unclipped the horrible dress from around my neck, baring my naked breasts. He put his hands on them, cupping them with great care. He squeezed them just as gently, and my head dropped back. He sprung up, and he started sucking my hardened nipples. He eyed me as he traced his thick tongue around the perimeter of my breasts to the areolas till he ended up flicking my nipples.

"Mmm. Cole," I whispered.

He kissed a trail from my breasts to my neck, and tingles rained over me. It sparked a fire within my belly for him. I suddenly had a memory come to me of a group of women in a river, naked and free, dancing around in the icy waters. It titil-lated me as much as Cole was doing as he continued to lick my neck. He licked my ear lobe, and I moaned as he stuck his tongue in my ear.

"Do I turn you on, Violet?" he asked in his sexy baritone.

My inner girl squealed. I took a shaky breath. My mind fixated on the hardest part of his anatomy rubbing against me. I remember glimpses of it the last time we were together. I bit my lip harder than expected, but I wasn't to be outdone. I trailed my finger along his hairy muscular pec, over his six-pack. I placed my hand over his hardness and looked into his eyes. He stared into mine.

"Do you know what to do with it?" he whispered.

I raised my eyebrow this time, but I nodded. On a whim, I leaned toward him and slowly licked his lips. He opened his mouth almost immediately, and our tongues intertwined in the air. It was the most erotic thing I'd ever done so far, and a shiver rippled through me. I pulled away from him.

His sexy blues were darker, smoldering fires of their own. I gracefully stood as I began to move my body to a sensual beat in my head. Drums thumped, and I gyrated to the rhythm. As I danced, I closed my eyes and peeled the revealing dress from my body. I opened my eyes when it lay on the floor at my feet.

"Where'd you learn to dance?" he asked.

I frowned because it was there one second, then gone the next. "I don't remember."

He smiled reassuringly. "Don't worry, baby, we'll make you more memories. Come here."

I took a step, but I still had on very tiny panties. I looked at him and smirked.

"Come get me," I said.

He gave his own grin and stood to his impressive height. He proceeded to me, but I held up my hand to pause him. He stopped, giving me a questioning look. I backed up a few steps.

"Down," I said, pointing to the floor. I waited to see if he'd play with me. It took a few seconds for him to understand.

He sunk to his hands and knees, awaiting instructions.

"Good. Now come get it, Wolfie," I said.

He crawled to me slowly. As he closed the distance

between us, I got wetter and wetter, waiting to see what he'd do when he reached me.

All too soon, he was next to me. He craned his neck, grabbed the tiny panties with his mouth, and pulled them down my trembling thighs. I stepped out of them. Sitting back, he nuzzled my mound with his nose. He looked up at me and reached out suddenly, grabbing my leg. I was so surprised I gasped. Then he shocked me again by putting my leg over his muscular shoulder. My eyes widened when he parted my folds and began licking my nub.

"Jesus! What are you doing?" I moaned.

He pulled away to give me a sexy smirk, "Pleasuring you."

He bent to apply more pressure, and this time something began building deep within me. My legs were melting. I was sinking deep in this sinful sensation, and soon I couldn't breathe. I couldn't blink. I couldn't do anything but drown in the warmth emanating from my center.

"God! God!" I cried out with a voice that had never come from me. My legs trembled like I was being electrified. "God! Cole, yes, right there!" I licked my lips as the sensation ebbed.

My head was light, and I swayed, but I was soon picked up. He laid me on the bed, switching to strip himself. He took the time to peel his pants from his powerful, muscular legs. His body was unreal, like it was carved and not living. And he wasn't wearing underwear. He frowned and grabbed his thick, long dick. It too, was a work of art, and I wondered how the hell he got that thing inside of me. I licked my lips.

I motioned for him to come closer. He strode to me, holding himself. I got the craziest idea of emulating that slut Seraphina. He stood beside the bed, and I wrapped my hand around his warm member. I eyed it as a slightly darker shade than his tanned body. There was a sheen on the tip. Curious, I licked it; the taste was peculiar as I couldn't place it. Cole inhaled through his nose.

"Do you know what you are doing?" he asked.

His baritone would make my legs shake again, but I kept it together and nodded. He smiled but said no more.

I opened my watering mouth and pulled him into it. I tried to remember what Seraphina did; then I moved back and forth. Cole gathered my hair into his large hands and pulled it off my neck. I gripped the base and increased my speed.

"God Vivee, keep going!" he encouraged.

I slid back and forth until my mouth tired, so I pulled him out. I licked the length of him, proceeding to the tip. He shuddered, closed his eyes, and tilted his head back. I put him in my mouth again, sucked gently, and pulled back slowly.

Cole snapped his head up so fast I jumped. He pulled his hands from my hair and pushed me on the bed. "Lay back, I have to have you now!"

I relaxed, and he climbed on top of me. He began situating himself but stopped and eyed me with a frown. "Vivee, did he have sex with you?"

"No!" I said.

"Good, I plan on snapping his neck. I want to do it for the right reasons."

It was on the tip of my tongue to tell him then about the dream, but he parted my legs and slid inside of me. I couldn't do anything at that point but grip his shoulders and moan. He moved slower this time, but he raised my legs higher, and the sensation was maddening.

"Oh God, Cole! Mmm yes! Yes!"

The bed rhythmically knocked against the wall as he moved, and I didn't care at this point who overheard. I rode that wave again as it ebbed and flowed. That burning, melting sensation assaulted my mound, and I urged it closer to me. Cole bent his head and kissed me. While his tongue ransacked my mouth, I trembled with waves of pleasure. My tongue tussled with his as well. He picked up one of my legs, put it on his shoulder, put a hand on the wall above my head, and drilled into me.

I had never experienced the feelings that filled me then, but Goddess help me I hoped every time would be like this.

"God, Vivee, you feel so wonderful, baby," Cole whispered.

"Mmm, Cole, you feel good too," I said.

He suddenly stopped and pulled out. He turned me on my side and lifted my leg, entering me again. Surprisingly, he closed my legs. He started thrusting again.

"God, yes! Fuck me!" I cried.

"You have a foul mouth, young lady."

"Yes, and you love it."

He smiled and winked.

I couldn't believe I could still feel anything other than him, but butterflies swarmed my belly. I ran my hand over his body in a frenzy as that familiar synergizing began in my center.

"Mmm God! I'm coming! Jesus!" I suddenly gripped Cole's forearms as a loud moan erupted from my lips, and my body melted. Soon after, Cole uttered his own growl. He panted and fell next to me. He reached out and grabbed me in a bear hug. I nestled in his sweaty arms, blissful and satisfied.

Hours later...

"How do you do, lass? The name's Cassius, but you can call me Cass. No need to fret, I haven't taken a drop from a human in centuries—strictly animals," the vampire assured me as we stood outside Cole's hut. I extended my hand and experienced the coolness of his pale skin, offering a friendly smile.

"Pleasure to meet you," I responded, diverting my attention to Cole as he bid farewell to the clan. Tears flowed from some, while others expressed wishes for a safe journey. Women embraced him tightly, and children clung to his waist.

"It'll only be a short while. Rafe will look after you all," Cole reassured them.

Under the radiant sun, Lindy had prepared a bag of essentials just for me—clothes, toiletries, and some of her handcrafted items. She insisted I accept a necklace her husband had given her, and despite my attempts to decline, she pressed it into my hands. Her blessing came with a warm kiss and a tight hug.

A sensation of being watched prompted me to turn, discovering the elder named Magnus fixing me with an enormous smile. With the aid of his cane, he hobbled over to me.

"Beginnings and endings, my dear, are always bittersweet," he remarked upon reaching me.

"I don't mean to take him away," I expressed, a hint of remorse in my voice.

"The Goddess knows what She's talking about. The unity of the people will be needed, and you two will usher it in," Magnus assured me.

"Do you not see me as a stranger? An outsider?" I couldn't help but inquire.

"A stranger is merely a friend you haven't met," he replied, his feeble shoulders lifting in a shrug. "I want to show you something." He produced a folded paper from his pants and handed it to me.

Unfurling the delicate paper, I found a map. "Is this Evernite?" I asked.

He nodded. "The entire expanse. And it was there," he pointed to a location on the map. "I discovered this." Placing pictures into my hands, I observed ancient walls adorned with inscriptions. One image featured a crescent moon, its curve resembling a gentle smile.

"Oh my God!" I exclaimed.

"Hey, that looks like your tattoo, Vivee," Cole remarked.

I glanced up at him, noticing a furrowed brow as he peered over my shoulder at the picture. He reached over to grab it for a closer look.

"Let me see that," Cassius said. Cole handed it to him, and he examined it for a moment. "This is the mark of the Witches of the Glades. They're an ancient coven rumored to have gone off the grid a while ago."

"Off the grid?" I asked, my forehead creasing with confusion.

"Yes, meaning they were part of society, and then they weren't. No one knows where they went. You're a witch? Cool," Cassius remarked.

"Witches of the Glade?!" I murmured.

"You're a witch?" Camille asked with a smile. Everyone started murmuring.

"Yeah, sorry. I know the rules..."

Camille made a gesture with her hand. "That's ok. We already like you."

I looked at all the smiling faces eyeing me. I smiled back.

Magnus addressed Cassius with a chuckle. "Very good, young man."

Cassius joined in the laughter. "Please. I am older than you."

Magnus simply laughed and nodded.

"Well, baby, what do you want to do?" Cole inquired.

I blinked rapidly. "I guess we go there to see what we can find."

"Hmm. It'll take days, and we must travel through several factions of lands to get to where those photos were taken. But if you guys are up for it, I am," Cassius said, his grass-green eyes studying me.

Cole gazed at me, and I let out a sigh before nodding. He enveloped me in a tight hug and slung both his pack and mine over his robust shoulder.

The community accompanied us to the edge of the compound, near its back. As we stepped into the woods, the people stopped and waved, and we turned to reciprocate. Despite the excitement of the impending journey, I couldn't help but smile, realizing how much this community had become a family to me.

Child, protect them, a voice echoed in my head, and I almost didn't recognize it.

I don't know how, Mother Moon, I replied.

Feel the magic; it is rife within you. Bless them, and I will bless you, she promised.

I opened my hands, spreading them out. A surge of energy coursed through my body in a flash. I envisioned everyone safe within the compound, any potential threats becoming confused and lost in the woods before reaching them. My hands warmed with the energy.

"Vivee, look!" Cole exclaimed.

I opened my eyes, and all eyes were fixed on the clear dome that now enveloped the lands. Cheers erupted from the children and villagers alike. With a sense of accomplishment, I lowered my hands.

"Good job, that'll keep them safe. You're amazing," Cassius complimented.

Cole embraced me once more, planting a tender kiss on the top of my head. We exchanged one last wave with the community before gazing toward the forest, ready to press forward. We were venturing into the unknown, but that was nothing new in my life. The path ahead led through treacherous territory, across foreign lands. I couldn't predict who we'd encounter or what challenges lay ahead, but with Cole by my side, I felt confident that we could face anything life placed in our path. We would face it all together.

Thank you

<u>THANK YOU FOR READING</u>

Now that you've read the novel, please leave a review on your favorite online retailer. I appreciate all of you and want to know what you think.

Sneak Peek

Here is Eclipse of Fate:
Book Two of the Lunar Prophecy Series

CHAPTER 13

The Calm Before the Storm

Cole

They say you can't cheat death, but I'm living proof that fate has a twisted sense of humor. I never believed in second chances until the day I rose from the dead, the rules of life and death be damned.

It began over a week ago - she walked into my life and altered my destiny. I saw myself as an uninspired leader, observing life from the sidelines. But no longer. Now, blessed by the Moon Goddess with a mate, I fought and perished for her. I slew a brother and lost two of my pack yet reclaimed my honor with the Blood Moon Brotherhood—my clan.

My name is Cole Wilderwolf, and I am a werewolf.

In the past, we stuck to tradition, married our own, and rejected outsiders. That included other werewolf factions. We were a proud people, but like all proud and, dare I say, arrogant people—we were very wrong. Then I found... her—hurt, alone and scared. How could I turn her away? How could I abandon that beautiful face and those lovely purple eyes? Purple, you ask? Yes, so enchanting she was named for them. Violet Belladonna.

When the collective dictated I turn her away, I refused. Though it meant betraying all I once held dear, one look from those violet eyes crumbled my prejudices. Some called me traitor, but in Violet's arms, I found acceptance––and a love more authentic than any I'd known.

"Cole? You ok?"

We stopped in a secluded forest clearing, having kept to the woods to avoid detection. I gazed at my love and smiled. Her beautiful black hair was piled atop her petite head, exposing her elegant neck. Her usually pale skin glowed with a hint of color. She smiled back at me, her expression speaking volumes.

"Yes, just thinking love. Where are we?" I asked.

"The map says The Muted Thicket." She scrunched her dainty nose. "I wonder why they call it that."

"It holds secrets, lass. A good many peddlers come through these woods," Cass said. I turned to look at the only vampire I'd trusted––so far––Cassius Greythrone. He was paler than Violet, with grass-green eyes and blonde hair. He kept himself meticulously clean.

The freshwater river gurgled as I refilled both Violet's and my flasks. The clearing filled our noses with the scents of fresh grass and earth. I took a deep swig of the cold, refreshing water to quench my parched throat. I passed the flask to Violet and watched her sip. The lowering sun then caught my eye. The cicadas had already begun their evening song.

"Let's make camp for tonight," I declared. "We can continue at dawn." I furrowed my brow and eyed Cassius. "How can you walk in daylight when the others cannot?"

"We've traveled together for three days, and only now, you

ask?" he retorted with a smirk. "I kid, lad. Years of practice and an enchantment allow me to brave the sun. I dread the dark. The boogeyman terrifies me."

Violet giggled, and I grinned. "But the boogeyman is just a story we tell children. He's not real, right?"

Cassius tilted his head. "Lad, things exist beyond the ken of nature, man, or beast."

"What are you not telling me, Cassius?"

The vampire sighed. He pulled a blanket from his pack and spread it on the ground. Then he sat. "When your kin was possessed, he wasn't just possessed. He was ripped from his body and soul. No going to the spirit world to be reborn. It was as if he never existed."

"What could do such a thing?" Violet asked. She sat near the bank of the river, and I sat next to her. We both faced Cassius.

"During my travels, I heard of an unholy entity that trumps all evil. Its name is The Umbramortis. At the beginning of time, it sought to feed off the misery, pain, and loss of beings. See, back then, lads, things were a lot more turbulent. People warred over land and ownership of people, and there was no helping it. Brother against brother. Children against parents. It was chaotic," Cassius said.

"Wow!" Violet said, turning to look at me. She caressed my face. "I'm glad I wasn't there. It sounds horrible."

"Are you sure?" Cassius said.

Both Violet and I looked at him, stupefied.

"I've said too much. We should get some firewood. It might be cold," Cass said.

"The fire can wait. You can't simply drop a bombshell like that without explanation," I said.

"Look, lads, all I know is I have been tracking events that have hinted this thing is coming back. It led me to you. And then I dreamt of Mother Moon, and she told me to aid you as much as possible," he said.

"What's in it for you?" I asked.

"Oh, my story is for another time. Come, we are running out of light. We should move swiftly." He walked off into the woods.

I stood and helped Violet to her feet. We set off too: me collecting wood while Violet carried it. I readily took it from her when it became an armful, and we turned around. When we arrived, Cassius was lighting what he'd gathered. I deposited our firewood. And Violet, carrying a pack with our provisions, started pulling out our dinner. Cassius being a flask of buffalo blood we'd acquired yesterday. He'd killed it cleanly, and the way he blurred when he moved fascinated me. We'd lain out the meat for jerky, and it was so big we still had some. We'd also gathered various vegetables, and I arranged them on the fire to cook them.

We were all seated, preparing for another night of Cassius's tales of adventure, when I heard those fateful footsteps. Cassius heard it, too. He stopped talking, moving fast, but in the firelight, he was simply a blur in the forest's inky dark.

I sprang to my feet to protect Violet, prepared to change into wolf form at any moment. But Cassius soon returned from the darkness with a woman. He restrained her with his sharp fingernail pointed at her throat.

I frowned, confused by the anger on Cassius' face. Something told me he knew this woman and didn't like her. "Who are you?"

"This bitch, is Sybil Nightshade. She's a seer. *The* seer for Evernite and her revelations *always* come true," Cassius muttered.

Want to read more? This book will come out three weeks following book one. Stay tuned to when the book comes out by visiting my website or stay up to date with my newsletter. Visit www.janaewritesbooks.com to find out more.

About the Author

Janae is an emerging author of dark fantasy romance. Janae's family is from Louisiana and Georgia. She is the middle child of three. She began her writing career as a teenager in high school writing steamy love scenes for her classmates. She wasn't convinced as a writer until her English teacher found her stories and told her she should be a writer. She treasured those words for all her adult life.

She has a bachelor's degree in information technology. She is a dedicated mother, friend, and writer. She is usually found hunched over her laptop dreaming of different ways to entertain. Her hobbies are video games, painting and writing poetry. She lives in Georgia with her cat Persephone and son.

She loves dogs and wants to own a Siberian Husky. She feels happiest making people laugh and feel comfortable. She has a podcast called How Not to Write with Janae and her favorite color is blue. Her favorite authors are (the late) Jackie Collins, Sarah J. Maas and Anne Rice. Her favorite genre is dark fantasy romance, but she reads anything with a hook. She is a Cancer with Sagittarius rising.